DIARY
OF A
YUPPIE

LOUIS AUCHINCLOSS

▼

DIARY
OF A
YUPPIE

▼

1986

HOUGHTON MIFFLIN COMPANY

BOSTON

Library of Congress Cataloging-in-Publication Data

Auchincloss, Louis.
Diary of a yuppie.

I. Title.
PS3501.U25D43   1986   813'.54   86-2870
ISBN 0-395-41649-3

Printed in the United States of America

S 10 9 8 7 6 5 4 3 2 1

*A signed first edition of this book
has been privately printed by
The Franklin Library.*

For
CHUCK KADES
The Greatest Lawyer
I've Ever Worked With

DIARY
OF A
YUPPIE

· 1 ·

I HAVE BEEN WORKING such long hours on this last corporate takeover that I have hardly made an entry in my journal for six weeks.

And right now I pull myself up.

Is that what I have finally decided this is? A journal? After all these years? That whole file drawer that I keep in the office — away from Alice's too curious eyes — the accumulation of jottings on long yellow foolscap: letters written but unsent, "personalities," imagined dialogues, remarks I wish I'd made at parties (staircase wit), diatribes of hate, hymns of love, endless dissections of my own fears and neuroses — could they all have been gradually melding into a form, a shape, a journal? And just what is a journal? A novel with a narrator, an "I"? Henry James disapproved of these; he said that they limited the tale to what the narrator could observe. The greater drama, according to him, was to see the observer observing. But people know more about themselves today than they did in Mr. James's time — or at least they should. And they certainly know more about themselves than even their closest intimates know about them. Or again — they certainly should.

My first papers go back a dozen years to my undergraduate days at Columbia, where I majored in English, as the best preparation for law. There are bits and pieces of stories and novels, for there was that brief period in freshman year when I actually contemplated becoming a writer. Soon I gave up the idea because there are too few financially successful writers; the law has a much broader peak. But I suspected even then that I was going to use pencil and paper on some kind of regular private basis to maintain my mental balance in a world populated by humans obsessed with their own illusions. For surely most people live more in their own fiction than in their own fact. Fact is too thin, too dry, too small, too passionless. And they? Why they, of course, are great tawny roaring lions — at least in their own mind's eye.

But it is time I stopped meandering. That is, if I am really to follow the aim and drift that I think I begin to see emerging from the yellow mass in the locked file cabinet behind my desk on the fortieth floor of the Pan Am Building. A journal I have just now called it, and a journal, for a time at least, it will be. I am writing at home tonight, but I shall be sure to put this paper away in my pocket before Alice comes in from her Metropolitan Museum lecture. Alice would never go through my pockets, but she would not hesitate to read anything I left around. She plays the literary agent at home as well as in the office and insists that I have a book in me. Or is that just an excuse for vulgar female curiosity? But is male curiosity any less vulgar?

I suspect that what may be orienting my words now on the yellow page before me is my suspicion that the new crisis in my office life is not an ordinary one. Like a good lawyer, let me state the facts, or what Mr. James would call the donnée.

"I" am Robert Service, aged thirty-two, an associate in the law firm of Hoyt, Welles & Andrew (thirty-six partners, a hundred clerks), and I have been privately assured (not guaranteed — they never do that) of my ultimate promotion on the first day of this coming January, 1980. Partnership has been my sole ambition — you might even call it my obsession — throughout eight years of driving work, including most weekday nights and many weekends. And what do I feel, now that triumph is nigh? Very little.

I have become a specialist in corporate takeovers. The one I am working on now, under Branders Blakelock, is the bitterly contested bid of Atlantic Rylands to take control of Shaughnessy Products. We represent the aggressor (I use the word advisedly), and the "target" is engaging in every defense of the game, including the "scorched earth" policy of encumbering its properties with debts and long-term leases to discourage the predator. It is also starting up new lines of business, closely allied to Atlantic's, so that the latter may be faced with the menace of an antitrust suit in the event of victory. In such warfare all is fair.

Or should be. Mr. Blakelock is my problem. It has come about this way. A routine procedure is the search, sometimes through paid informers, for evidence of improper conduct of the officers of a target company. Armed with such a find, one can sometimes blackmail the target into a compromise or at least, by means of a derivative stockholders' suit, get rid of a troublesome officer. Examination of "abandoned property," a euphemism for the contents of the target's trash baskets, is often rewarding. Mr. Blakelock finds these tactics offensive, and I try to shield him from awareness of them, but I had to tell him about one shredded document, which we had pieced together, to get his permission to bring a suit against Albert Lamb, Shaughnessy's president.

It was a memorandum from an accountant to the company treasurer about Hendrickson Lamb, Albert's younger brother, an alcoholic with a sinecure job and a salary paid by Albert personally. The interesting part of the memorandum dealt with what appeared to be an embezzlement of company cash by the brother. The memo read: "As you know, it is Mr. Lamb's practice to refund such defalcations promptly from his own account."

So there it was. Perhaps not much, but enough to start a stockholders' suit seeking the removal of Albert Lamb from Shaughnessy. And Albert was causing Atlantic's biggest headache in the attempted takeover.

I knew that I should have trouble with Mr. Blakelock, and I waited for some time this morning for the right moment to break it to him. He had called me to his office to discuss a motion in the federal District Court that I am to argue next Monday. He has great confidence in himself as a coach and likes to imagine himself as an impresario, a kind of Svengali who can inspire or even hypnotize a disciple into a brilliant performance. I always sit patiently and silently through these sessions.

Indeed, I hardly look up at him. It is enough to sense him towering above me, standing tall and bony in one of those baggy black suits that he has worn throughout the eight years I have known him, booming or shrilling alternately down at me from the mahogany lectern at which he likes to stand as if he were some Abelard of old preaching to students.

"And remember, Robert, when you have finished your oral argument, don't trail off, or glance at your notes for some afterthought or final emphasis, but obey the immortal command of the late John W. Davis, the greatest pleader it was ever my privilege to hear" — here the reedy voice becomes suddenly stentorian — "and *sit down!*"

But this morning I am tired of it. The job has been too long and grinding, and it is not half done. The knowledge that I should soon be a partner has not brought the anticipated ecstasy but instead a quickening anxiety as to whether I have chosen the right firm. Of course, I have always been like that; foretasting is so much of my satisfaction that I rarely enjoy even a brief elation upon fruition. It seems to me that I am weary at last of Blakelock's paternalism. He has liked me, preferred me, perhaps even loved me. I have to some extent made up for the son he has never had, and that has been a fine enough thing while I was an aspiring clerk, but now that I am ceasing to be a clerk, should I not be promoted to the more equal status of younger brother?

That has a rather nasty look, even to my eyes, as I reread it. Imagine how it would seem to Alice! But was it my fault that Blakelock chose to crowd me into the vacuum of his heart? I have always liked him — I still do — but he ought certainly to understand — who better? — how much it has been to my advantage to play along with a senior partner who has my destiny in his hands. Why do people persist in the illusion that their caring creates some kind of duty of reciprocation, or even respect, in the hearts of those they care for? Why do they kid themselves that there is something fine or noble or duty-creating in the fire of a passion that they have not only deliberately kindled in themselves but have huffed and puffed on to make it as large and crackling as possible? How many of them ever seriously try to douse it? They don't because they're afraid they might succeed. And they don't want to succeed any more than they want to face the fact that the object of their affections is usually the creation of their fantasy.

For what am I, Robert Service, to Branders Blakelock? Not what I seem to myself, anyway. I cannot be sure, obviously, just how he likes to picture me, but I hazard the guess that it may be as an Antinous on whose bare muscular arm the wise old leader of the ancient world does not disdain to lean. Should that not be enough for

Antinous? What is he, poor Bithynian lad, if not the beloved of Hadrian? I do not suggest that Blakelock has lascivious designs on me — nothing, I am sure, would shock him more, even in his most secret thoughts — but I do note that his protégés have all been handsome, and we know what a cesspool the subconscious can be. Or, to put it more innocently, perhaps he conceives of me as a kind of faithful wolfhound, crouched submissively at his side but ready at a signal to leap, to rush, to kill.

"Remember, also, Robert, that Judge Axeman, like so many of our federal bench, thinks of himself as a man who can change the world. While the president and Congress are paralyzed by party faction, *he* will ensure that discrimination shall be abolished, if he has to bus our youth a million miles a day; that votes shall be equal, if he has to redistrict all our states; and that the environment shall be preserved, if he must bring industry to a grinding halt! God bless him — I'm half on his side. But what, you will ask, can a reforming judge expect to accomplish in a corporate takeover? Is it not a case of two scorpions in a bottle? Perhaps. But remember that behind every judicial idealist there lurks a lover of power. Axeman likes to play with our big companies as a boy with an electric train. And that is where your role comes in. You must make him feel that the takeover of Shaughnessy Products is a more efficient way of distributing the loaves and fishes to the multitude! You must help him to don the toga of the public servant. Precedent must bow to the general welfare — that is, when precedent is against us!"

But I have heard it all before. Looking down the long oblong sparsely furnished chamber — two rather fine English cabinets, a Colonial bench and some wooden uncushioned armchairs, signed photographs of judges on the walls and "spy" cartoons of British lawyers — it strikes me that litigation has survived in a world of computers like a Toonerville trolley on the track of a Metroliner. Yet its very survival has made it curiously revered. The tricks and winks and chuckles of the courtroom technique, the voice of thunder, the sly insinuations, the throat clearings, the whispered conferences, the whole hammy vaudeville adored by judge and jury — and by television audiences — has become too sacred to be touched, has even in some crazy way taken the place of our empty churches as the shrine of the oldest American virtue.

It is now that I choose to blurt out my discovery about Lamb. It is not the right moment — it is never the right moment — but at least I have his attention.

"Where the hell did you dig that up?"

I hesitate. "Do you have to know?"

"I suppose it was an 'abandoned property' search? Very well, don't tell me. I don't want to know. You're surely not planning to use it?"

"Of course I am. I plan to use it as the basis of a suit to remove Lamb as c.e.o. of Shaughnessy."

"You've got to be crazy, Bob. I knew about Al's brother. He's a kind of kleptomaniac. Al has always looked after the poor nut."

"Nut? Has he been judicially declared incompetent?"

"Of course not. Al was much too proud. He handles his family problems himself. He's supported that brother all his life and put his son and daughter through college. He even manufactured a kind of career for him in Shaughnessy, at his own considerable expense. I never heard of anyone who did more for a sibling."

"But a brother's hand in the till is still a crime, isn't it? And isn't Albert's covering it up another?"

"I suppose, technically. But it can all be explained."

"Can it? And even if it can, would Albert Lamb like the exposure?"

"Hell, no! It would probably kill the poor loon of a brother."

"Then there you are. Albert will have another inducement to settle. Isn't that what we're after?"

"Robert, I can hardly believe my ears. Is it really you talking?"

"Do you suppose Albert Lamb would think twice before using a weapon like this against any officer of Atlantic?"

Blakelock has to pause at this. "Well, you have to remember that Albert feels that Atlantic is trying to destroy his very lifework in Shaughnessy. A man in that position gets pretty desperate. But you and I are not in that position, Bob."

"Our client is. Atlantic has very high stakes in this case. What can we lose, Mr. B, by taking the chance?"

"Nothing, I suppose, but honor."

"Where is that? Didn't we check it when we went into the takeover business? Why don't you let me try it, anyway? There's nothing like one bit of dirt to start up another. People hearing about the case may suddenly remember more. We may dig up enough dirt about Lamb to blow up his whole board of directors!"

"No! Never! I won't have it!"

His indignation makes me bold. "You talk about honor. What about duty to a client?"

"Can you really believe that it obliges me to pick up a tarnished piece of family gossip and puff it into a scandal that may destroy Albert's peace of mind and perhaps his brother's very life?"

"Why is that relevant? It's a fact, isn't it, that Albert Lamb covered up the crime of a junior officer? And isn't it our duty to use every fact at our disposal? Lamb knows that as well as we do. When he got into this fight he knew that everything in his past would be pored over and used. That's how the game is played, Mr. B, and what's more, I think it's basically how it was always played. Only today we're franker about it. And I think that's better."

"I think it's worse. Much worse. I think it's obscene, and there's no place in my law practice for obscenity."

In the silence following this I look up at last, intending defiantly to meet my boss's eyes. But he has turned his back to me, and his shoulders are stooped with what strikes me as a rather melodramatic expression of dismay and grief.

"You'd really sling that kind of mud, Robert?" the sad, now deep voice rumbles at me.

"I'd sling any mud I could make stick. Albert Lamb is the key to the whole defense."

"Even admitting it's mud?"

"But legal mud, Mr. B!"

"I had not been aware that mud observed these distinctions."

"Why shouldn't it?"

"Robert, you appall me. You would really, for a dubious advantage to a client, so bespatter your adversary?"

"You mean it would be all right if the advantage were less dubious?"

After another solemn silence Mr. Blakelock speaks with a faint note of weariness. "Let me put it very simply, then. This material will *not* be used."

"Can't we think it over for a day or so? Give me a little time to convince you."

"I'm not going to change my mind, Robert. The material on Lamb's brother will not be used by this firm in a derivative stockholders' suit or in any other way. I am no longer concerned about that. What concerns me much more is your amorality. It comes as a sad surprise to me. I feel almost as if I did not know you."

"Have you ever wanted to know me?"

"Go home, Robert! Go home before I lose my temper! Take the weekend off; stay away from the office. Tell your darling wife what you have told me and listen carefully to what she says. I miss my guess if she will not agree with me. Let her help you, my boy. Let her guide you! I fear I must have been a false leader."

"Mr. Blakelock —"

"Go home, son, go home! I've had enough of you for one day."

· 2 ·

OH, YES, I have a very definite feeling that this crisis is not going to pass. I may find myself making a significant addition to the file drawer of my penciled fulminations. What a crazy collection it is — hundreds of pages of myself recording or imagining my talks with others! Before I married Alice I even used to write love letters to girls I hardly knew, or didn't know — sometimes to movie stars — which of course I was never mad enough to mail. When I was angry with people I would write down all the terrible things that I wanted to happen to them or draft legal documents dealing with their arraignment and condign punishment. I wrote out my dreams in the most copious detail and learned not to blush at my daytime erotic fantasies. I think I have learned the hard lesson that it is perfectly possible for a man to know himself if he will only accept the premise that he is probably not very different from his neighbor.

Only yesterday, for example, I encountered my fellow

clerk, Glenn Deane, on the steps going down to the 77th Street subway stop. He was out of tokens and asked if I had an extra one. There was a long queue before the booth. I said I was sorry, that I had only one. In fact, I had four in my pocket when I left him to stand in that queue.

Now what am I telling myself? That Glenn would have done the same thing? Not necessarily. His own form of meanness may not embrace subway tokens. But I am confident that it embraces many larger things. It so happens that I buy twenty tokens at a time, and that I like to see how long they will last me. It is a kind of game, or perhaps the vestige of some ancestral miserliness; I may enjoy the clink of "golden" tokens in my palm. Yet I would willingly lend Glenn a thousand bucks, which is considerably more than he would ever lend me. This goes to show, not that I am more generous than Glenn, but that meanness is not measured by the amount withheld. We are all mean about something, which means that we are all mean.

Take another example. The other day, again in the subway with Glenn, I emitted a silent but smelly fart. I could see by Glenn's puckered nostrils that he had noted it, and by a glance at a stout black woman standing before him and a shrug, I managed to shift the blame. Thousands of people do that kind of thing. It is not nice to do them, but it is better to face the fact that one does. I used to be ashamed of being scared in airplanes, and when I ceased to be ashamed, I ceased to be scared. As a matter of fact, I usually take care *not* to fart in the subway.

Which all means that I believe I have occasional insights that some of my nearest and dearest lack. I certainly think that I know a good deal more about Mr. Blakelock than he knows about himself.

To describe him. At sixty-nine Branders Blakelock is a tall, spare, ungainly man, bulging and tightening in the wrong places, with a high bald dome surrounded by a fringe of curly gray hair and a smooth bland face with small, shiny, twinkling blue eyes. His voice, which can be stentorian in court, is also capable of high, almost falsetto notes, and he has an exploding, cackling laugh which would be almost an insult were it not largely used to applaud his own sharp wit. He is brilliant, and he knows it and is not in the least ashamed to show that he knows it. At the Irving Association, his favorite club, named for the sage of Sunnyside and of which he has been president for some years, he loves to address the membership, either informally at the long table where he is famed for his barbed stories of New York worthies, past and present, or at the monthly dinner meetings, where he reads out the obituary list, ending in sweet, mournful tones with the famous couplet of William Cory's:

> "They told me, Heraclitus, they told me
>   you were dead;
> They brought me bitter news to hear and
>   bitter tears to shed."

For Blakelock is very much a man's man. He is gallant with the ladies and pretends to be the slave of his dull, plain wife, but he really lives for his own sex, at the office pacing up and down his chamber and tearing apart the suggestions of his clerks, or at the Irving Club in the activities just described.

Is he a great lawyer? A great trial lawyer, perhaps. He is an unblushing showoff, sometimes soft, sly and humble, sometimes a thunderbolt-hurling Jupiter, but more often the mildly amused, gently cynical gentleman whose scholarly achievements and urbane sophistication never cause him to lose the common touch. He is a bit on the old-fashioned side, with a twist of Arthur Train's Mr. Tutt, the sharp old Yankee lawyer with the heart of gold, who beats the dirty shyster at his own game to save the widow whom the latter is trying to fleece. But the qualities that shine in the courtroom are less glowing in the conference chamber, where men are trying to get at the truth and not camouflage it. And as no big firm can survive on litigation alone, Mr. Blakelock must spend more hours in his office than in court. And I don't think he really likes it when he has to fool not so much other people as himself.

For that is what men toting a bag of puritan principles must do when they practice law. Hoyt, Welles & Andrew, like many of the old-time corporate law firms, had at first disdained takeovers as dogfights to be left to less reputable practitioners, but when takeovers became the principal indoor sport of American finance they had no choice but to learn the game or lose their clients. And it did not take Blakelock long to become as sharp at the sport as anyone else. But this has vexed him.

He has always, for example, been uneasy about the jargon of this type of corporate conflict. He either carefully avoids use of such terms as "bear hug," "shark repellent," and "blitzkrieg," or else articulates them with a sardonic and venomous precision. He detests my casual use of them. Here is a conversation we had at the beginning of the Atlantic-Shaughnessy affair, when I happened to use the term "golden parachute."

"Does it never strike you, Bob, that these labels may be the true moral indicia of what we are doing? Historians have always professed to find illumination in the vernacular."

"I don't find it necessary to decide."

"You just go ahead and do what you think you have to do?"

"Like you, sir."

"Oh yes, oh yes." The glinting eyes darken, and lumps of mucus change place rumblingly in the throat. "A job's a job. If you take it on, you do it. No one knows that better than I. But I suppose I'm cursed by an inner mentor that sits above the turmoil of my spirits and points out with glee: 'You're a shyster, Branders Blakelock. Or if you say you're not, will you kindly explain the difference?' There's no such devil in your heart, Robert?"

"If there were, I'd send him packing. Isn't that what you pay me for?"

"It's what we're making you a partner for — on New Year's Day next. But I'm probing you, my friend. Do you mind? I'm trying to discover if you can really be so happily free of the cancer of an inner judge. Have you *no* doubts? Even when you see the tail of the predator consuming its prey already clamped in the jaws of a larger predator? Does it not remind you of those chain-of-life charts where you see the otter eating the fish that has swallowed the frog that has gobbled the fly? Ugh!"

"Well, it's life, isn't it?"

"Perhaps you even like it." He has left the lectern now and taken a step closer to my chair as if to examine a curious object. I sigh with no attempt to conceal it. "Perhaps you conceive it to be a man's role. Macho, isn't that the term? With all that curly blond hair and those blue, blue eyes! Young America in a Will Rogers film. And yet isn't there something lean and hungry behind that mask? I know because I've made use of it, God help me! Maybe it's your generation. God is dead, and the frontier is gone, and there are no wars to fight, but a man must still use his fangs and claws. After all, there has to be *some* fun in life!"

"Look, Mr. Blakelock." I have always found it awkward to use his Christian name, though he has repeatedly asked me to. "I'm not responsible for the low price of common stocks. It's not my fault that there are companies that take advantage of the market to buy up other companies. I thought you believed in a free economy."

"I do. I do."

"Well, we're adjusting to it, that's all. And helping our clients to do so. Why make such heavy weather of it?"

"Because it seems such a travesty of the American dream!" Now he is pacing the chamber again, the great professor on the dais, peering from a murky past to a misty future. "The old robber barons at least covered our land with rails and factories. But their successors simply devour one another. We may all end up in the distended bellies of a few somnolent titans that will sit facing each other across the desert of our poverty like giant Buddhas, too gorged to do more than gaze with blurred eyes at their own navels."

"You forget the antitrust laws."

"They seem very resilient these days. Everything favors amalgamation. Even the computer, which is nothing but an instrument for reassessing what we already have. New ways of looking at the old. Our future has dwindled to a change of labels."

"Which reminds me that I must be getting on with changing the label of Shaughnessy Products."

"Right you are, my boy! Shut the old windbag up! You know that for all his prattle he's in this bloody business right up to his prating mouth!"

The raid on Shaughnessy was peculiarly obnoxious to Blakelock because Albert Lamb, the target's president, had been a member of his Saturday golf foursome at the Antlers Club in Rye. Because of the ironclad secrecy in which preparations for a takeover had to be shrouded, it had been impossible for Blakelock to give the faintest warning to his friend. Indeed, it had behooved him not to betray the danger by the least change in his normal attitude and behavior. Even a failure to appear at the first tee on any Saturday morning at nine might have been taken as a sign of embarrassment, and Lamb might have speculated: embarrassment over what?

How well I could imagine that last Saturday morning before the raid! The low, rolling, wooded, autumnal hills, yellow and brown and hectic red, the azure sky with here and there the puff of a cloud, the sweeping yellow-green course, and the four old boys in their tweeds, chattering comfortably (except for Mr. B) as they ambled along, on all the topics so dear to them, happy and secure in their male solidarity, free of the sharp words and possessive affections of the other sex.

Perhaps they were discussing the war in Afghanistan that has just started. All would have expressed outrage at the Russians, Mr. B with particular violence.

"The devil about the hydrogen bomb is that we can't afford to do the right thing. It's too dangerous. But at times I feel that if we don't take some chances, we're going to lose our souls as surely as the Soviets have."

"What do you suggest, Branders?" This perhaps would be from Lamb, gray-haired, square of chin and shoulder, an executive from a cover of *Fortune*. "Would you send in troops through Pakistan and call them volunteers?"

"Damn it, Al, I think I might!"

"But the Reds would send in ten men for every one of ours. It would be Vietnam all over again against a foe many times as strong. You have nothing to fight with, Branders!"

"It is recorded in the Scriptures that Samson smote the enemy with the jawbone of an ass." I can just hear Blakelock's high, snooty laugh. "So if you, my dear Albert, will oblige us by shipping your lower maxillary to the Department of Defense . . . !"

But now Blakelock would be going too far. He would

not be so acerbic if something were not eating at his heart. He knows that in a day or so an attack will be launched against Shaughnessy Products that will in all probability result in the ouster of his golf companion from a position it has taken him a lifetime's labor to achieve. What will Lamb think of him, knowing that on that lovely morning in the country, smacking the golf balls and talking of heroic stands in Asia, his supposed friend was actively plotting the raid that has destroyed him? And indeed Albert Lamb *was* furious and has since retired from the foursome. But Blakelock does not so much care what Lamb thinks of him; he is too big a man for that. What he really minds is what he must think of himself. That he, Branders Blakelock, a god of the Irving, a man of good will, a holder-up of the beacon light of good fellowship and humanitarianism, should find himself in a position that in the good old rosy past might have been described as more suitable to a legless, slithering reptile!

Yes, I feel sorry for him. I really do. But what I cannot get away from is that he is basically doing it to himself. He wants to be a leader of today's bar and at the same time reconcile his actions with a code of ethics for a *désœuvré* society of nineteenth-century aristocrats. And obviously it's not going to work.

· 3 ·

ALICE'S REACTION was very different from Mr. Blakelock's. Whereas he was concerned with my ethics, she was concerned with my relationship with him.

"Why do you have to be more Catholic than the pope?" she demanded. "If he doesn't like it, why not drop it?"

"Because I want this takeover to take."

"Isn't that his affair? You're not a partner yet."

"No, but do I even want to be a partner of a firm that hasn't the guts to do the job?"

"Guts? It's the first time I've heard you accuse Mr. Blakelock of not having guts."

"Call it fastidiousness then. His nostrils are too tender. One nasty smell, and he gags."

"One nasty smell! Ransacking garbage pails?"

"Of course, you would jump on that aspect of it. If you concede that information has to be gathered, you must go where it is."

"I guess I don't concede it has to be gathered."

"Why should you? You're not a lawyer. But leave the practice to those that are."

"I do! To Mr. Blakelock! I'm perfectly happy so long as you follow his lead. But now it seems you no longer do."

What man who calls himself that would not have been angered? To have it spat in my eye that my boss was not only my boss but my preceptor, and a badly needed one at that! As I looked at Alice, so tall and fine and proud and dark, it struck me that she and Blakelock were acting as if they had formed a secret alliance to keep an unruly boy under control.

"Maybe we'd better have supper," I equivocated. "Is it ready?"

"It can be ready in ten minutes. I want to go on with this first. You've changed, Bob."

"I haven't changed in wanting my supper."

"I tell you it's coming."

Alice was the perfect wife. She took pride in being ready for me whenever I came home. Our two girls had had their supper and were doing homework in their room. Audrey, who was eleven, sometimes supped with us, but not tonight. Alice would have left her office at five and come home to take over from Norma, our black cook–cleaning woman, who left at six, having prepared the meal, which only had to be warmed up. At seven, when I arrived, on nights that I wasn't working late, she was clad in a long dressing gown tightly belted, which admirably set off her tall, full figure. Alice was a dark beauty with pale skin and eyes that looked as if they would have betrayed laughter had she not been so determined to be serious.

Our living room owed more to her gravity than to her taste. I think Alice thought that interior decoration was trivial. There was too much blue on the sofas and chairs, and she had a cabinet of ornaments given her by a mother of middle-class tastes that contained statuettes of animals and birds. The walls had two Piranesi prints that had belonged to her grandparents. It was surprising that a woman of so much character could have produced a chamber with so little. But Alice was literary; her domain was words.

"You think you're always the same, Bob. But you're changing, little by little, all the time."

"In what way?"

"Shall I put it bluntly?"

"When do you not?"

"Well, then you're getting hard-boiled. Or perhaps I should put it that you're trying to get hard-boiled. As if you thought there was something desirable about being cool and clear and above it all and looking down on poor scrapping mortals."

"And there isn't?" But for all my jaunty tone, I was cruelly hurt. Who wants to be thought hard-boiled?

"No! Sometimes I wonder what happened to the blue-eyed, laughing boy who sat next to me at Columbia and collected the famous lines of English poetry that had clumsy mates."

" 'My heart is like a singing bird,' " I promptly quoted.

" 'Whose nest is in a watered shoot,' " she came right back at me.

" 'Match me such marvel save in Eastern clime.' "

" 'A rose-red city half as old as time!' "

"I could go on."

"Could you, Bob? When I see you day after day, night after night, so wrapped up in one of these ghastly corporate raids, I can't help but wonder."

"That's my job. The only difference between now and eight years ago is that now I'm making some of the decisions. When I was a junior clerk I had no responsibility. I might as well have been running the elevator. But I always knew the time was coming when I'd have my share. What else was I slaving for?"

"Was that really it? You mean you always imagined that one day you'd be doing this kind of work? And loving it?"

"Well, of course, I couldn't know I'd become a specialist in takeovers. But it was always going to be some aspect of corporate law. That's what being an attorney is all about."

"Even the dirty tricks?"

"Even what you call the dirty tricks. The trouble with you and Blakelock is that neither of you has the remotest understanding of the moral climate in which we live today. It's all a game, but a game with very strict rules. You have to stay meticulously within the law; the least misstep, if caught, involves an instant penalty. But there is no particular moral opprobrium in incurring a penalty, any more than there is being offside in football. A man who is found to have bought or sold stock on inside information, or misrepresented his assets in a loan application, or put his girl friend on the company payroll, is not 'looked down on,' except by sentimentalists. He's simply been caught, that's all. Even the public understands that. Watergate showed it. You break the rules, pay the penalty and go back to the game. Albert Lamb would do to any officer in Atlantic exactly what I propose doing to him. If not, he should be benched."

"So you think Mr. Blakelock should be benched."

"I'm certainly beginning to wonder about it."

Alice was fair enough to give to what I had said some moments of thought. But then she came, in her woman's fashion, back to the personal aspect. "I guess what I really mind is your enthusiasm about it. If you thought of it just as a job, that would be one thing. After all, it's not your fault that American businessmen are such sharks. But the glee with which you ferret around in ash cans! Why do you have to want to do so much more than Mr. Blakelock wants?"

"I've told you. He's old-fashioned. And I have to get ahead."

"Have to?"

"Well, do you think my family don't cost me a mint? It's all very well for you to spend your days with your poets and think high and lofty thoughts, but I notice that you expect private schools for the girls and that you like to travel and —"

"Yes, of course I do. You don't have to be a financial giant to have those things."

"But if I'm going to be anything, I'm going to be a giant. There's no halfway for me."

She sighed. "That's it, then. You want to be what you're making yourself. It's a free choice."

"And always has been. I haven't changed. That's where you're wrong. I could prove it to you in the papers I've kept."

She visibly shuddered. "You mean you might let me read them? After all these years? I wonder if I want to. Now."

"Because they might show you had married the wrong man?"

Our eyes met. "Maybe. Maybe that *is* what I'm afraid of."

If she had only burst into tears! There is nothing I would not have done for a weeping Alice. I have a recurring dream of Alice suffering some cruel and undeserved punishment, writhing, bewildered, clutching a rag about her exposed limbs as a savage tormentor strikes blow after blow upon her bare back. Alice hurt, terrified, pleading, desperate . . . ; I wake up and cry out aloud at this picture, as vivid as some nineteenth-century academic painting of a tortured Christian slave girl. At such moments I love Alice so passionately that I can imagine myself, like the Roman officer in *The Sign of the Cross*, tearing off my insignia and leaping into the arena to meet the lion's gory mane at the side of my love. A happy death!

But no. Alice always has to be above me. She has to be the angel of light. She seems almost able to divine the rush of my inner sympathy and anxious to head it off. I suppose she spurns it as sentimentality. But love is love, in all its forms. It is not to be lightly rebuffed.

· 4 ·

ALICE THINKS we have been drawing apart. We haven't. She has been drawing apart from me. And she thinks that we are becoming disillusioned with each other. We aren't. She is becoming disillusioned with me. I have the same opinion of her that I had when I married her, and I believe that my opinion is still a correct one. This is not because I am more perceptive than Alice. It is simply that I am not burdened with the astigmatism of her need to idealize people. She is not unlike Mr. Blakelock in this. As a matter of fact, she is not unlike many of our middle class in this. Her parents had the same failing and taught it to her. My parents also tried, but they were inept teachers. Any child could have seen through them.

When Alice and I enter a cocktail party, we tend to give the impression of a fine young American couple who will probably go to the top of their ladders, or fairly high up anyway, and who will grace those ladders in doing so. "What a fine pair!" people exclaim. We are both of a good size, well made, with little fat; Alice has rich dark hair, a squarish face, perfect skin, and her eyes, wide apart, bear an expression that combines, charmingly, a warm sincerity with a faint, pleased surprise that she is so continually being confronted with such wonderful things. And I, of course, as I have so often confided to these pages, am the all-American kid (the kid in his early thirties, however), who looks as if he would like nothing better than to bound out of the house and pass a football with his host's sons and who was probably freckled when he was their age. The great difference between us is that Alice supposes that the impression we give bears some relation to the actuality. I know that it's just an act, like other people's acts. That does not necessarily make it sinister. Are other people sinister?

If I were to tell Alice that I love her as much as I did on the day we were married she would probably retort that in that case I have never really loved her. But would it be true? What is love? She has never ceased to be physically attractive to me, and I delight in her sense of humor and respect her intellect when it is not clouded by illusions about love and duty. If she were a little more honest with herself, she would be almost perfect. It is a fact, as she complains, that I do not miss her when I go off on business trips, but then I never miss anybody when I know I shall see them again in due course. This is true of all but the neurotically dependent, but it does not make one popular to say it. Alice likes to make a great deal of missing me, but then she wants to miss me. She does not think she would be a deep person if she did not miss the man she loved. Or ought to love.

For love to Alice is a very big thing. She thinks that people who do not have it have missed the best in life. She does not realize that everyone has it. That might make it seem too cheap. And it has to be based on a solid pedestal of honor; true love, in Alice's book, exists only between two morally upright and mutually trusting persons, who should also have a generous political and humanitarian viewpoint. I should not go so far as to say that she believes true love exists only between Democrats or liberal Republicans in tune with the *New York Times* editorial policy, but there might be a kernel of truth in it. True love may be found between Romeo and Juliet, but never between Macbeth and his lady. And indeed if Alice is today beginning to see me as morally unworthy of a great passion, it is because she is building an excuse for its failure between us. It cannot be she who has failed in the challenge of love. That would be unbearable to her.

Alice and I were both only children. Only children are apt to be extreme realists or extreme idealists; it is obvious how that turned out in each case. And the reasons are also obvious. Alice's father was a man who considered that he was a failure when he was actually rather a success. My father considered that he was a success when he was actually rather a failure. The offspring of each reacted in such a way as best to protect themselves from a repetition of parental illusions.

The Jock Nortons, Alice's parents, lived down the

road from us in the village of Keswick in Westchester County. Alice and I were classmates in high school and later at Columbia, where we became engaged in our senior year. We were "childhood sweethearts," which Jock Norton always maintained was the American nightmare, only half laughing when he said it. He was a free-lance writer who always believed — according to Alice, for he was too much of a gentleman to say it — that, had he not saddled himself with a wife and child and an expensive house in the suburbs, he might have been a first-class novelist. What he never realized was that his genius was precisely for the kinds of pieces that he did write: brilliant short stories, witty satirical poetry, devastating movie reviews, which brought him a modest but regular income. He was better off, I am sure, lamenting a career as a major writer of fiction than facing its failure. Isabel, his wife, was saved from the boredom of suburbia by her constant anxiety as to whether her husband's regular drinking and irregular adulteries would get out of control. They never did. Jock Norton always knew what he was doing. He was a bit of a ham who was ashamed but not ashamed enough of being one. He even had the decency to be a bit ashamed of his success in playing the role of adored father to a too genuinely adoring daughter.

Fatuity, on the other hand, was the keynote of my father's life. Jason Service was and still is, at seventy, an associate in the great Wall Street firm of Burr & Doyle. When he started practicing law in the late 1930s that firm had perhaps fifty lawyers; now it has three hundred.

Dad's tall, ambling figure, his high, shiny dome, big nose and bleary gray eyes are almost a trademark of the organization. Everyone knows him; everyone respects him; everyone pities him. Why did he not move on when he failed to make partner thirty or more years ago? Because he had a specialty in patents and a safe little niche, and he always claimed that he was not interested in the "rat race for partnership," that there was adequate dignity and satisfaction in a job well done. He loves, or purports to love, his little nook in the law and insists that it is a relief not to be bothered with administrative problems or what he likes jocularly to call "ambulance chasing," by which term he simply means acquisition of the roster of clients necessary to support any law practice. He has always made a decent salary, and our small Queen Anne house and acre of land in Keswick are situated on a pleasant rural road. He could afford to send me away to Haverstock Academy for my last year of high school, so I was able to enter Columbia with some air of being a "preppie." And poor Mother, spare, thin, angular, apprehensive, has always been so fiercely defensive of him that I believe she has almost dreaded that my own incipient success might tear the blinders from his eyes as to what his own career has not been. She needn't worry. Deep down he knows. People always know.

My reaction to Father's position in Burr & Doyle was one of violent humiliation, all the worse in that I recognized that the truly shameful thing was my feeling so. Father and Mother were very well thought of in Keswick; their friends and neighbors would have been shocked by my attitude. But my trouble had begun at the age of twelve when I had the bad luck to see my father through the eyes of the snotty son of a senior partner. Mr. Doyle and Father were exact contemporaries and had started in the then firm of Burr & Hutchinson right after law school, even sharing an office. The rise of one to senior partnership while the other remained a salaried associate naturally put a strain on the friendship, but Mr. Doyle was not a man to let it too glaringly show, and he always affected a rather demonstrative heartiness towards Father when they met. Once, when we were asked to a firm outing at Mr. Doyle's estate in Roslyn, Long Island, his son Tom was delegated to take the lawyers' children on a ramble in the woods. Walking in the lead with me he asked me my name. "Oh, yes," he commented when he heard it, "you're 'Old Jake's' son. My dad says yours is one of his top clerks. 'They don't make 'em like Old Jake anymore,' he always says. 'They broke the mold after they made him.' "

Oh, the compliments of children! That one broke my life in two. I thought of Father from then on as a kind of Uncle Tom, and I should not have been surprised to hear that the usually benevolent Mr. Doyle, chancing to find his faithful servitor in some breach of duty, had brought the lash down on his stooped shoulders. To my parents' dismay I refused ever again to go to a firm outing, becoming almost hysterical when pressed. And when I graduated from law school I hurt my father deeply by declining even to be interviewed for a job in Burr & Doyle, although Mr. Doyle, impressed by my grades and *Law Review* editorship, had been genuinely anxious to offer me one. But I knew that David Burr, Jr., had just been taken in as a partner, and I would rather have died than give people the chance to quip: "Burr & Doyle is the only firm in town with a father and son among the partners and a father and son among the clerks!"

Now who would have said a thing like that? Very likely nobody. But the fact that I knew that my soul was the only one on fire did not make the suffering less acute. Indeed, the only thing that would have made it more acute would have been precisely if others *did* suspect it. Alice, for example. She might have left me had she known that I was ashamed of my father, whom she adored. But then Alice's mind is as different from mine as day from night. She may hardly realize that Dad is *not* a partner!

· 5 ·

ATLANTIC RYLANDS has lost its bid to take over
Shaughnessy Products, and even though it has made
millions out of its defeat because of the boosting of
Shaughnessy shares it had to acquire, the feeling among
its officers is bitter. It is an instance of money not being
everything; victory can be more coveted than profit.
One vice president went so far as to imply to me that
Blakelock's friendship for Albert Lamb had signally
reduced his aggressiveness. What would this officer have
said had he known of the unused opportunity of Lamb's
brother!

"Frankly, Bob," he told me, "there were some of us —
and I don't mind including the chairman of our board
— who wish you'd been in charge."

"Oh, come now. Branders Blakelock is one of the un-
disputed leaders of the New York bar. He's taught me
everything I know, and I'm still learning."

It was loyal of me to say this, but loyalty is a quality

that is highly regarded in corporate circles. A young man who turns on one boss may turn on another.

"He may be a leader of the old bar, but this is a new one. I don't really believe that men of his generation have what it takes for this kind of work. They're too bogged down in old ideas of politesse. Like that French officer in the history books who invited the enemy to fire first."

"I guess you have to have been born after World War II to be a real skunk."

My friend grunted appreciatively. "And I guess you need one to fight one."

I have been giving the most serious consideration to the question of whether or not Hoyt, Welles & Andrew is the right firm for me. I've been compiling statistics, breaking the partners down according to age, social background, religion, inherited wealth, law school, competence and legal specialty. I am troubled particularly by their ages. Nineteen out of thirty-six are over fifty and six are over sixty-five, which means that the next echelon will already be old by the time they take over management and will tend to lack the vitality and keenness needed to fight cases of increasing toughness and complexity. As a junior partner I could not reasonably expect to have a determinative share in executive decisions for at least a decade, by which time the firm might be down the drain. For we have seen grand old firms fall apart; it is a known thing.

And how do I feel as I write this? As I face the fact that I may have spent eight years of exhausting work in

the wrong law firm? I think what I feel is actually a kind
of excitement! What is it but a great challenge, and one
that I already begin to make out a way of meeting? At
least it is more interesting than much of what is contained in my daily grind. And suppose I lose? But I shall
not lose.

The key to my solution is going to be Glenn Deane.
Glenn is thirty-five and still an associate, though he has
not yet been passed over, for he started late as a lawyer
in the firm, having first been employed as an accountant
who studied law at night. He is brilliantly able, but his
partnership is not fully assured, as he is not considered
"attractive" by some members of the firm. And indeed,
he is *not* attractive. He is big, but on the stout side, and
he is very plain, with a cauliflower nose, pushed a bit to
the left, pockmarked cheeks, an oval chin and clever,
mocking, small greenish-brown eyes under a high brow
and balding dome. But he makes a bold and abrasive use
of his unattractiveness, converting it into a kind of rough
sex appeal. He knows when to wheedle and cajole and
when to be brutal, even a bully. He is quite untrust-
worthy and capable of maudlin self-pity, but he can also
be devilishly funny, and at weekend gatherings at his
house in Chappaqua he is the life of the party, except to
the occasional guest whom he tears to bits, egged on and
applauded by his heavy, devoted wife, to whom he is
periodically unfaithful. Glenn has worked with me in
takeovers, and he is resourceful, imaginative and perfectly ready to use any weapon that he finds to hand.
With someone of my "polish" to make up for his lack

of it there is almost nowhere that he might not go. So we shall see.

He and his wife, Lynne, have asked us to spend Saturday night at their house in Chappaqua. They are giving a cocktail party and have suggested that we may not want to drive back to the city before Sunday morning. Norma has agreed to stay with the girls, and Alice has reluctantly consented. Reluctantly, because, understandably, she dislikes the Deanes. But she is always a good office wife.

Alice has been on a be-nice-to-hubby kick ever since the collapse of the Atlantic bid. I think that even she has been able to take in the gravity of one of these affairs when the client is dissatisfied, and she is troubled that she may have gone too far in criticizing my "aggressive" tactics. And of course she did go too far. She was pulling me down while I was trying to earn the money that she likes to spend. But I can overlook this because I love Alice and consider her a wife of great character and charm. She is an asset in my life, in my career, in my bed. And I suppose in my soul, if I have one. But I must also record that I gain an advantage over Alice if I abstain from open recrimination and allow her sense of guilt to work for me. And an advantage is something one can always use over a spouse. The occasions do present themselves.

The weekend of the Deanes' party is over.

Their home in Chappaqua is an old white farmhouse reduced to a half-acre of land by the encroaching suburb

and containing enough bedrooms for five little Deanes.
Lynne Deane is a noisy, stout blonde, efficient, direct,
unimaginative and easily hurt, frequently reduced to
despair by the cleverer but malign spouse whom she
resentfully worships. Unlike Alice, who stands aloof
from office gossip, Lynne knows everything about
everyone in the firm, and she loves or loathes them in
exact proportion to their being aids or obstacles to her
husband. Needless to say, she is a veritable cesspool of
gossip, and Glenn occasionally flies out at her savagely
for going too far. "Do you want to ruin me, woman?"
he will bark at her, and she will shriek back at him and
then storm out of the room in a torrent of tears.

Their cocktail party, which lasted for four hours, was
made up half from the office and half from the neighbor-
hood. The office people talked exclusively with one
another, and the neighbors did the same; we formed two
distinct groups, both perfectly content. Alice, following
her old-fashioned notion that a guest should "help out"
her hostess by cultivating strangers, did her best to talk
to the neighbors, one after the other, who would each
regard her with a faint suspicion and then resume their
gossip with one another. At length she gave it up and
joined me, like the other office wives who, whether from
timidity, boredom or lack of social initiative, tended to
remain glued to their husbands for the whole evening.

I make a habit of currying easy favor with Alice by
agreeing with her that these parties are tedious and insisting that I attend them only in the interests of good
office feeling. Yet the fact is that I enjoy them very

much. I like to drink, and I have a strong head; I relish
the mild humming in my temples aroused by seven or
eight gins. It never interferes with my concentration
on the revelations of my usually inhibited fellow associates, both male and female, as they open up under the
influence of alcohol. This sounds as if I were spying on
them, but it is more than that. A law firm becomes the
bulk of one's life if one gives oneself to it — and one
must do that to get on — and it is only sensible to want
to know all one can about one's own life. We always
start by talking shop at these parties, but after a few
drinks we get on to personalities, and that is when I learn
things. And why not learn things? What kind of a sot
would want to spend his life in a pit before a lighted stage
and never go behind the scenes?

Glenn at last took Alice away from me into another
room. He had drunk a lot; he may have tried to pinch
her, I don't know. He has rather a thing about her, but
Alice can take care of herself, and she never bothers me
with these things. But when the guests had at last de-
parted, and the Deanes and Services sat down to ham-
burgers and red wine, Lynne gave my poor wife some
undeserved dirty looks.

Our topic of discussion was Paul Merton, one of the
tax partners, a handsome, youthful-looking man still on
the sunny side of fifty, who was thought to have
jeopardized a career launched twenty years back with
his marriage to a senior partner's daughter, by his leaving
her now for a young female associate. His unfortunate
wife was an object of pity among the partners and scorn

among the clerks. The topic was of inexhaustible interest to the entire office family — with the exception of Alice.

"It shows there *is* something stronger than ambition, after all," Glenn observed. "As a young man Merton would swallow any shit to get ahead. But in the end Eleanor's huge ass and stringy tits proved too much for him. He had to find something gamier."

I dared not look at Alice. Glenn was always crude, but after drinking he became impossible.

"Was it that his ambition had its limits?" I inquired. "Or simply that it had been achieved? For what can his elders and betters do to him now?"

"They can block him from being senior partner."

"I wonder. How long are these things remembered? And Mrs. Merton is a born loser. People don't sympathize forever with losers."

"She's served her purpose and now can be cast aside," Lynne Deane commented grimly. "Merton's like a husband in old China selecting a concubine. I suppose his wife is lucky not to be thrown down a well."

"He's even making her go out to Reno for the divorce," her husband added. "Because he's too busy to take the time. That's really rubbing the old girl's nose in it."

"Then why does she do it?" Alice demanded indignantly. "Has she no pride? Or if there has to be a divorce, why can't she get it right here for adultery?"

"As *I* certainly should!" Lynne cried, glancing across the table at her husband. "If I found myself in her shoes!"

"Why, Lynne," I remonstrated gently, "we thought you supported Glenn in everything."

"Not in that department! It's hard to imagine any woman crawling so low. Do you suppose Merton has something on her?"

"You mean, does *she* have a lover?" Glenn demanded with a hoot. "Another associate? Surely that would revive my flagging faith in the supreme force of ambition. For if Paul could bring himself to Eleanor's mattress twenty years ago without gagging, think what kind of a boar it would take to mount her today!"

"No, no, she gave in for the good of the firm," I hastened to explain, uneasily aware that Alice was perilously close to an explosion. "The good lady did not want the partnership that bore her father's proud name to be mixed up in a sordid domestic relations case."

"A case of being too proud to fight?" Lynne sneered.

"Or was it really to do her poor bastard of a husband in," Glenn suggested. "What could more appeal to his outraged partners than the spectacle of a wronged wife bearing her woes in dignified, stately silence? And not stooping to besmirch the office they all adore? May the good Lord spare me from the malice of so sanctimonious a bitch!"

"I really cannot sit here and hear you say such horrible things about poor Mrs. Merton!" Alice had at last erupted; her face was paler than ever, but her eyes glowed. "To me she has always been far too good for the lawyers with whom she has had to pass her life. She strikes me as someone high and noble, a kind of proud

Roman princess in the late days of the Empire. She might have had to oblige her imperial father by giving her hand to a barbarian chief, an Alaric or Attila, whose bloody sword was needed to bolster his tottering throne. Oh, it's very fine! And how is she rewarded? Just as one might expect from a vulgar and ruthless killer!"

Alice seemed elated; even she, usually so abstemious, was feeling the effect of the prolonged cocktail period.

"So that's how you see us all," Glenn mused. "As a bunch of barbarians. Well, I guess we've asked for it."

"Well, do you ask for anything else?" Alice continued boldly. "Do you ever ask yourselves, 'Is there a life after partnership?' What will any of you have at Merton's age but some little cutie?"

"And Glenn damn well isn't going to have that!" Lynne cried hoarsely.

"Who's going to stop me, I'd like to know?" her husband roared. "If that's all the reward there is, I'll be blowed if I don't have it! Don't worry, Lynne. We'll get a young gladiator for you. We've agreed those barbarians can stomach anything." Here he shouted with laughter, and his poor wife was obliged to take it as a joke. "But what was so great about your Romans, Alice? Think of all those banquets and debauches!"

As Alice's eye involuntarily turned to the living room with the unremoved litter of the cocktail party, Lynne, finding an object on which she might vent her wrath, cried out, "Are you comparing our party to a Roman debauch, Alice?"

But it was not necessary for Alice to reply. Glenn, who had for some time been becoming angrier with his wife, decided to bat her down.

"Holy God, Lynne, you don't presume to compare your squalid little suburban cocktail affair with the glorious decadence of the lords of the ancient world! Wake up, woman, and try to see what I am faced with, day after dreary day! Forgive me, my friends, if I embarrass you, but there are moments when I cannot but scream at age and custom for not withering or staling my wife's infinite middle-classitude!"

Lynne, her hands on her mouth, stumbled from the room, and we heard her heavy steps and sobs as she stamped upstairs.

"She'll sleep it off and be fine in the morning," Glenn assured us casually. Alice at this retired in disgust to the guest room, which was on the main floor, protesting that she, too, was tired.

Glenn loved to sit up late, drinking whiskey, as did I. Besides, I had my plan. While I now proceeded to relate to him the results of my analysis of our firm, department by department, he remained very still and somber. From time to time his hand would, as if automatically, raise the dark drink to his lips.

"And what is your deduction from all of this?" he demanded at last.

"That the firm is on a downward path that is probably irreversible unless both the present and immediately future managements are replaced. And managements are not disposed to replace themselves. Of course, the decline could be long. It could be like the Roman Empire of which we were speaking. But declines have a way of accelerating."

"They do indeed. And when you and I are partners we'll be too junior to arrest this one."

"Precisely."

"So we're in the wrong firm. That's great. Where do we go from here? The big firms won't employ laterally. They like to train up their own partners. I suppose we could find a corporation. Or even a smaller firm."

"Or start our own."

Glenn took a deep breath; he was too concerned now even to swear. "Go on."

"There are fifteen associates working on the Celebes antitrust case. The consent decree is due any day now. The firm won't lay them off — it's too gentlemanly for that — but we know there isn't enough work for them all, and some are bound to be looking around. I think we might line up the whole bunch."

"And they're the cream of the firm!"

"Except for thee and me."

"But what about the cost of a new firm? The library, the computers, the space. Do we get all that from a bank?"

"No. From Peter Stubbs. *If* he joins us, and I think he will. He got millions from his old man. I'm sure he'll stake us."

"Jesus! You have got it worked out."

"But I've told no one. You're the first. I want you to think it over closely in the next week. If we decide to strike it must be worked out in advance: just what associates will go with us and what clients we can take. But I'll tell you one thing. I think we can start with a promise of one major suit for Atlantic Rylands. It should pay two years' rent."

Glenn whistled. "What will Blakelock say? I'd hate to be the laundress who gets his underpants after he gets that message."

"Blakelock is going to yell his head off. He's going to shriek and scream about treason and honor. They all will. But they've had their chance. They've taken our lives for eight years, night and day, and now they offer us a place on the bridge of a sinking vessel. If they would allow us to be the pilots, even now, I might stay. But no — we must go down with them. It's *sauve qui peut!*"

"Oh, don't misunderstand me, pal," said Glenn, rising to replenish his glass. "I'm not in the least concerned about those old farts. I agree that anything they get, they've begged for. But you're going to have a hell of a row with Alice, unless I very much miss my guess. She worships old Blakelock. She was telling me so only tonight."

"Alice will certainly be a problem. But she will be only my problem. And perhaps my only one. And she'll have to go along in the end. What else can she do?"

Glenn and I wrestled with our project into the small hours. I continued to enjoy the prospect intensely.

Indeed, I felt so excited at one point I had to go out to the porch to cool my flushed countenance in the night air. Now why should I have derived such pleasure at the prospect of putting into action a plan that might backfire and result in my finding myself not only unemployed but unemployable? Have I ever been one to court danger? No! Certainly not if there is danger of death. One of my nightmares as a boy was that I was living in the age of dueling and passing a sleepless night before having to meet my adversary in a deserted park on a chilly dawn and risk a bullet through my heart because he had chosen to misconstrue an innocent joke at a party. Whenever things go badly in real life I try to console myself with the thought that at least I am not being burned at the stake or eaten by big cats in an arena or shivering in a trench full of vermin in the hell of the first world war. I have an imagination easily inflamed by horrors. But when the penalty is not physical and where there is a reasonable chance that victory in the game will go to the player who is most skilled, then I find it high and exhilarating sport to gamble for high stakes.

When I went at last to bed I found Alice awake and reading.

"I couldn't sleep," she said. "I feel I've been unfair to you. You work hard and then come home to face my preaching. And when we come out here and have to stay through that ghastly party, I don't know why I assume it's all so much harder on me than you. Of course, you have to do these office things, and of course you don't enjoy them any more than I do! But you don't get snippy with Lynne Deane; you have the patience of an angel!"

As I went to the bathroom to get into my pajamas I reflected that the last thing I was going to do was to admit to Alice that I had enjoyed the "ghastly" party. I was going to need every bit of credit that I had with her; I couldn't afford to waste a smitch.

"Don't worry about Lynne," I told her as I emerged. "I thought you were very patient with her. God knows she *is* impossible. And of course you were fine with Glenn; he was ogling you all night. That's what peeved her."

"He's much worse than she is, really. She's coarse and ill-tempered, but her heart's in the right place. But he's mean, Bob; he really is!"

"Anyway, I thought you looked stunning. You were certainly the belle of the ball."

"Oh, darling, you're being ridiculous. And I love it!"

Alice was in one of her melting moods, anxious to make up to me for all her criticisms, seeking, as she sometimes did, to drown her doubts and misgivings about me in her memories of the blue-eyed idealist she thought she'd married. I knew that I should have to make love to her, and although I was tired and wished we could put it off till the next night, she was indubitably beautiful and so ready for love that she wouldn't mind a performance somewhat impaired by whiskey.

So we made love, and it was well enough. Why does Alice think it is cold and hard of me to understand her and wonderfully passionate of her to misunderstand me? If she would only stop to study the nature of love she would realize that I do love her. And that there may even be some doubt about what she feels for me.

GLENN AND I were agreed that we would have to move quickly to win over the four key associates of the group of fifteen that we proposed to detach from the firm. By the time we should have secured this vital quartet the project would have begun to leak, and it would then be essential to have an airtight plan, including the necessary financing, before the firm began to fight back.

It has gone so far with astonishing speed and luck. Atlantic Rylands has privately promised me a large retainer, and Glenn has received commitments from two important corporations. Three of our four key associates have responded with enthusiasm, and the fourth, Peter Stubbs, has agreed to give it serious thought. Stubbs, of course, is actually a cornerstone of my plan. He has recently inherited four million dollars from a toy manufacturing father, and Glenn and I have elected him to be our banker.

What about the morality of our lining up clients while still acting as supposedly loyal clerks of our old firm? Without question it is improper, but this gives me no trouble at all. It is universally done, and no one who knows the practice of law in America today carps at it. It is considered bad for a partner to do it — though this rule, too, is widely breached — but we are not partners. I have been virtually promised a partnership, it is true, but that is not the same thing. Any more than an engagement is a marriage.

Since entering the above I have had my crucial lunch with Peter Stubbs. It also went well. Peter is a dark, moody, rather handsome man who regards the world with an apprehensive eye that seems to be always questioning its motives. Were people after his money? Did they really respect him for himself? Would he not have to be tougher than the next guy to keep the next guy from finding him too soft? I suggested that he needed a cocktail, knowing that he would not take one. Then I ordered one for myself, so that I would be on a lower level. I wanted him to feel superior.

"If you made partner at Hoyt Welles, Pete — and you would, I'm sure — aren't people going to say you made it because of your old man's estate? But if you come with us, they'll know you're on your own."

"How is that true if I take Dad's estate with me? Be frank, Bob, isn't that the real reason you want me?"

"No! Leave the estate with Hoyt Welles. Everyone knows Al Hoyt was your dad's oldest friend as well as his lawyer. It would create a smell to take it away from him."

Peter now allowed a frank surprise to permeate his almost sullen expression of habitual reserve. "You mean you'd give up that fee?"

"We're planning a brand-new firm with brand-new business. We don't need a bunch of moldy old estates and trusts!"

"And you want me for ... for ... ?"

"For yourself, old boy!" I finished for him exultantly. "For the smart, hard-hitting shyster that you are." I reached over now to strike him smartly on the shoulder.

It was really too easy. Peter's gratitude was almost pathetic. I shall not even have to ask him to buy the library now, or pay the first year's rent. When I tell him to sign, along with the other new partners, our loan application to Citibank, he will at once see the advantage of becoming his own creditor on easier terms.

"Bob, I believe we're going to be everything you say!" he exclaimed. "I think I will have that drink, after all."

We now have six Hoyt Welles associates, including Glenn and myself, "pledged" and our first year's expenses assured. When will the thing begin to leak? For when it does, it will rapidly become a flood that may sweep us all away before we've signed up the other eight. But it won't, *Deo volente*. That is, assuming there's a God and he wills it.

Well, it is out now. And it has gone well enough, in one respect, if horribly in another. Horribly for me, anyway.

I learned of the discovery of our "plot" from Blake-lock himself. I still don't know how he discovered it but I suspect Glenn Deane's loud mouth.

I heard the unusual click of my door being closed and looked up to see my boss standing before me. His face was drawn, but there was an odd twinkle in the eyes that he fixed on me. I had to infer that it was a sinister twinkle.

"May I sit down, Robert?" He did so without waiting for my answer. "I have come to congratulate you on the formation of your new firm."

"I wonder if you can possibly understand why I had to do this to you, sir."

"Oh, I think I can." Blakelock removed his pince-nez and rubbed his eyes forcefully, as if he were trying to dislodge some intrusive object beneath the eyelids. "I have given the matter considerable thought since I learned of it two days ago. I even took yesterday off to play golf alone and ponder it. You younger men must see me, I concluded at last, not only as a man who is out of date but who is a hypocrite. You hear me invoking the ideals of the past while trying to garner the profits of the present. It is not an attractive picture, and I at first resisted it. I think I even at last rejected it. But that is not the point. The point is: do *you* honestly believe it to be true? And I concluded that you do. So that putting together a law firm *in petto* out of our employees while ostensibly working loyally for us becomes the only logical course of action to protect yourself and others."

I had imagined the various reactions that this crafty

old man might adopt or even simulate: righteous indignation, thunderous denunciation, withering sarcasm, icy silence. I had not anticipated this particular brand of humility, and my heart seemed to miss a beat as it struck me that it might augur a real danger. A pathetic, self-blaming Blakelock could put me in an ugly light in the business community. If he was going to wail and beat his chest, crying *"Mea culpa"* and "My son, my son," would our orderly withdrawal from his firm not take on the appearance of a ruthless raid?

"I was going to come to you, of course, sir, when our plans were complete."

"You mean, when it would be too late for me to take preventive action?"

"That is one way of putting it. What I was really afraid of was your power of persuasion. You may be surprised to hear it, but I feel that I owe you a lifelong debt for all you have taught me."

"I am surprised to hear it. Surely I did not teach you to dismember a law firm which, in its trust and naiveté, had offered you a partnership."

Ah, that was better! I thought I could make out the gleam of something like hate in that eye. "No, sir, you did not teach me that. I simply did what I thought I had to do, as you yourself have just put it. But because of my great affection and respect for you, because of all my obligations to you, I feared that I might not be able to resist any urging on your part that I abandon my plans."

"Your affection and respect for me, Service?" Blakelock's tone rose shrilly now, but almost at once he caught himself up. Was I wrong in suspecting that he had flared my eagerness to have him take an angry stand? "Well, I suppose people have different ways of expressing those feelings. I daresay there will be those who will criticize you with some harshness, but you and I know how rapidly even the sharpest criticism in this city dies away. Particularly if your new firm is successful. As I'm sure it will be."

"We have modest hopes, sir."

"No doubt. And of course you will keep a watchful eye on your young employees. You will know of what they are capable."

I smiled at this, but my smile was not returned. "Well, I see that words tend to bitterness," he continued. "And I have no wish to be bitter. Let us turn to the practical details of our severance."

But it was when I came home that night at nearly ten o'clock, after both girls had gone to bed, that I discovered that, if my life had taken a brave step forward in one direction, it had come to an ugly halt in another. Alice was sitting on the sofa in the living room without a book or a drink or even a cigarette. She had obviously been sitting there grimly, waiting for me to come in.

"Blakelock called you?" I surmised.

"He came to see me. This afternoon. In my office. He suspected that you would not have told me. Perhaps that you had not dared. He wanted me to have his version of what happened before yours."

"In case I should color it?"

"On the contrary, he wanted to present what you had

done in the light most favorable to *you*. Or perhaps I should say, in the light least unfavorable."

"With what purpose?"

"He seemed to be afraid that if I heard it as you would tell it, I might pick up and leave you."

Alice looked very bold and white and handsome as she said this, and I began to feel the tremor around my heart of what I knew was going to be rage.

"So he purported to justify me?"

"He tried to make me see you as representative of your generation. He wanted me to understand that what you had done was not an unusual or even a dishonest thing according to the mores of your contemporaries."

"And did he convince you?"

"He did not. I still believe that you behaved like a skunk."

When I spoke at last after this I tried in vain to keep the rasp out of my voice. "Does that mean that you *will* leave me?"

Alice chose not to answer my question directly. Instead she rose and crossed the room to the fireplace and pointed to the chair opposite the one in which she seated herself. It was suddenly a kind of formal interview.

"I have got to do some thinking, Bob. About us. Some very serious thinking. I realize now that I've been putting it off for at least two years. I've had a growing suspicion that you are not the man I thought you were. I don't suppose that is your fault. Except that you may have tried to pull the wool over my eyes. Indeed I fear you are still trying to do so. But now I must learn to see you as a man who is willing to plot in secret to dismember the law firm of his loving and trusting benefactor. A man who considers it a smart piece of business to kick over the ladder that he has so dexterously climbed. A man who takes an unholy pride in putting daggers to the only use he sees for them: plunging them into his neighbor's back!'"

She might have been the avenging angel of my childhood dreams, stern, impassive, without pity, without mercy, a Gustave Doré lithograph. She seemed to be viewing my cowering nudity with an eye too cold for contempt, gathering behind that high, brooding brow the comminations of parents, teachers, a whole generation of elders. How they all scorned my vulnerability, my irredeemable sleaziness! But I was no longer a boy. What had life and long labor done if not to arm me against the savage injustice of their assault? If I was Satan conspiring against the heavenly host, was this not the confrontation that I had always known was bound to come?

"I don't suppose it would do me any good to defend myself before so prejudiced a tribunal. You have been so snowed that there's no longer any hope of finding much brain under your false morality. How can you be such an ass, Alice? You're like my father, an Uncle Tom, broken by a system he failed to dominate, who now prates about his honor and dignity. As if he had either! And if Blakelock believed half the things he pretends to believe in, he'd be a public defender. But of course he's everything *you* admire. As opposed to a poor fool of a husband who works his can off to earn the money you're willing enough to spend!"

"I guess I'd better stop spending it, then," Alice replied firmly. "I must learn to be on my own. And if that means I must live alone, I must live alone. For a time, anyway."

"Where will you go?"

"I'll get a room somewhere. Or stay with friends."

"And then I suppose you'll get yourself a smart lawyer and go after a big settlement!" I had to pause here to swallow; my throat was dry, and my temples were throbbing. "But let me tell you something, sister." Yes, even in my excitement I recall that I heard myself use that vulgar term! But it was too late; I had to push on, noting the gleam of contempt in Alice's eye. "If you think you'll get a penny out of me, you have another think coming." How could I use such language? But I did! "You have no grounds for divorce or separation. I have never been unfaithful to you, never struck you or abused you, never failed to support you. I've been a good father and husband, and you are leaving of your own free will. I doubt you'll even get alimony *pendente lite*. I shall fight you every step of the way, for the girls, for my money, for my home!"

"I shall ask nothing of you. I shall support myself."

"You won't find that so easy," I sneered.

"I'll manage somehow. I assume that you'll pay for the girls and allow me to visit them here until I can afford a place of my own. We can work all that out. I've never criticized you as a father."

For a moment my heart was ripped apart. How could

I have lost this splendid girl? And if she saw me as a good father, which I certainly was, and not as a good man, was she possibly not right? Was it too late to undo the whole ghastly mess?

"Alice, don't be an ass!"

"Isn't that what you just said I was?"

"If you walk out on me, you'll give me grounds for a separation. Don't put yourself in that position. Or at least talk to a lawyer first."

"I appreciate the warning. And I realize it's not one that you would normally give a potential opponent. Thank you. But I don't care what advantage I afford you. Lawyers had nothing to do with our coming together. And so far as I'm concerned they shall have nothing to do with our coming apart."

All my ire returned with her complacency. It even irritated me that she should take it for granted that I would give her no trouble as a father! Why should she assume so blandly that, mistreated as I was, I would not use any weapon in my arsenal? Actually, she was being an irresponsible parent to risk her own custody of her daughters!

"I'm warning you, Alice. If you leave this apartment, you'll be breaking the deepest compact that can exist between a man and a woman. I cannot guarantee how I may change as a result. I may turn into an even uglier person than you think me. I may charge you with all kinds of things in court and claim custody of the girls. You may find yourself without money and without a family."

"That's ridiculous, and you know it." Alice rose at this as if to terminate the interview. "What could you possibly do with two daughters, keeping the work hours that you do? You'd end up offering me a salary as their governess. But in the meantime I'll come here in the evening after the office and have supper with the girls and help them with their homework. We can arrange the weekends later. Who knows? Maybe I'll be back in a month's time, begging you to take me in! But I've got to try something else, Bob. I really do. And now we've said enough for tonight. It's been a terrible strain."

"You don't show it."

"I don't always show things. But it may comfort you to know I have a splitting headache. And I'm going to bed now. In Norma's room." The maid's room in our flat was occupied by Norma on the infrequent nights when we were both away. "I've already moved my things in there."

"Alice!"

"Please, Bob. It's enough for now. Really."

And so, in a few wretched minutes, a life can be torn in shreds. I took a bottle of whiskey to the strange, hostile solitude of our bedroom.

· 7 ·

My life has become such a furnace of work in the organization of my firm that I have not been able to maintain my comforting and consoling habit of entering comments in my journal. It seems to me that I have been nowhere except our new offices on Lexington Avenue and the apartment, where I try to see my girls at least once a day. I have almost lost the power to think except about the problems of my happily successful new law practice. And yet for all the nervous tension there have been rewarding moments. Sometimes at night when both girls are doing their homework and I allow myself a couple of stiff Scotches, my heart actually pounds with exultation. I am pulling it off. I am creating a law firm. By God, I am really pulling it off!

But now, after reading over the last paragraph, I find I must qualify my statement about exultation. It is all very well for a man to talk about the delights of loving his children, but if he cannot confess to himself that the protracted company of two little girls, however bright, however darling, does not have its tedious aspect, he is a self-deceiver. And, of course, it is also true that I bore the girls. They begrudge me the time that I spend asking them perfunctory questions about their friends and school (knowing that I am not really interested), just as I begrudge them the same time taken from office affairs. The closest families are not necessarily those that see most of each other.

I suppose I must admit that Alice has been so quintessentially the heart of our family that the girls and I find we do not have much of a relationship when she is absent. It is she, after all, who maintains the genuine and constant concern in all details of the girls' daily lives and who keeps the jokes and the chatter bubbling when we are all four together. I can never seem to remember the names of their friends or teachers. Indeed I had better confess at once that I like to hug them and kiss them and leave it at that. Or at most watch them playing with their friends in Central Park when I am sitting on a bench and have a book to read. It might have been different had I had sons, but I am not even sure of that.

For example, Audrey the other day wanted me to read a blotchy one-page paper that she had written for school on Pizarro and the Incas. I knew that she only wanted my approval. I have learned that in homework children wish the parents either to do it for them or praise what they have done. I'm afraid I did neither.

"I've never seen why explorers get so much space in history books," I said. "If they hadn't got where they got, someone else would have, the very next year."

"Miss Lake doesn't care about explorers. She calls them 'exploiters.' She says what Pizarro did to the Incas was cold-blooded murder."

"But that's the way the Spaniards did things. If Miss Lake doesn't like it, why does she want to read about it?"

"Because it's history, Daddy! And she teaches history. That's her job."

"Well, I don't believe in making snap judgments about historical figures. You weren't there. You don't know all the facts. Or even a fraction of them."

Audrey was as pretty as her mother, but her nature was conventional and little open to new ideas. Sally, her junior by two years, was square-headed and down to earth.

"There's no point talking to Daddy about homework," she said flatly. "He doesn't think like the teachers."

I usually manage to be out of the apartment when Alice comes; our talks are few and brittle. She tells me that her literary agency business is going well and that she needs nothing. This probably means that her parents are helping her. I am beginning to realize that I shall have to pay her something if she stays away permanently, but I am still betting that she will be forced to return. I know that her parents cannot afford to support her indefinitely.

My mother has now settled the matter. When I came home last night I found her in quiet charge of the apartment and the girls peacefully eating their supper.

"Leave them be, Bob," she said firmly. "Mix yourself a drink and listen to your old ma."

Mother, so forceful, yet so thin and plain and gray and somehow immortal, never subject to weather, time or emotion! I have always thought of her as weighing me in the balance and finding me wanting, perhaps because I seemed somehow to threaten Father, or at least her image of him. Yet I never feel that she disapproves of me, or even that she does not love me. It is more as if I were in some strange fashion too much for her and that she has always been fair enough to blame herself for this more than she does me. I have perplexed her, but is that, her troubled look seems to ask, my fault?

"The way you're living is no way to live. You can't look after the girls and work the hours you do. You've got to let Alice come back and live in this apartment while you get a room somewhere."

"But this is my home, Ma!"

"Alice is a bargain. She'll look after the girls and the apartment for free. You'll save money on a housekeeper. And you needn't worry about the legal angles. Your father, at Alice's insistence, has drawn up a document by which she waives any rights against you for leaving this apartment and renounces all claims to alimony. He hated to do it, but she made him. So you see, nobody's trying to trick you out of anything. We just want to get on with our lives, that's all."

I felt that I was being put in a very shabby position. Everyone else, it was being made to appear, cared only for the welfare of my daughters while I was standing on a bundle of petty legal rights. And yet I was being quietly done out of my home, wife and offspring!

"I don't see what right Alice has, deserting me, to expect such favorable treatment."

"She has no rights. She's not expecting anything. I'm the one who's arranged it all. I've talked to the girls, and they want their mother back. They love you, Bob, but you're never home."

"Is that my fault?"

"Fault? Oh, you lawyers! Look here, my child. You're up against four women, and you haven't a chance. Do what you're told and be thankful."

Mother had a point. I was licked, and I guess I was glad to be licked. Today I moved to the Stafford, and Alice came back to the apartment. I suppose it may be a relief at last to be able to devote all my time to my firm. God knows it needs it. And the acrimony between Alice and me is now much reduced. Having her back in the apartment may pave the way for our reunion.

·8·

IT HAS NOW BEEN six months since I made the last
entry in my journal. Managing a successful and rapidly
growing law firm has taken most of my time, the bulk of
my energy and just about all that has been left of my
heart. At this writing we are seventeen partners and
thirty-nine associates, and we have to take additional
space. With a couple of years' hard work and a continuation of my lucky streak we should become one of the
major corporate law firms in the city. Stranger things
have happened.

It has not been easy, nor has it been without the
shattering effects on my personal life to which I will
duly advert. The main trouble, in the office, has been in
establishing myself as the administrative head of the
firm. The crying need for a strong executive is not
always recognized by lawyers. There is still some survival of the old-fashioned notion that a "real" lawyer
will be so absorbed in his practice that he will tend to be

restless at any administrative restrictions imposed by his office. Lawyers who despise problems of management as petty and distracting invariably regard themselves as having a larger vision and greater souls than those who do not. In sober truth they are more apt to be selfish prima donnas, indifferent to the suffering and inconvenience to their staff caused by chaos in maintenance.

Glenn Deane was my principal opponent in this. He has sought to establish his own little firm within a firm, treating his "faithful" junior partners and clerks to limousines and first-class air tickets, allowing them to keep irregular hours and, worst of all, surrounding himself with a miniature court that laughs appreciatively at his sneering cracks at "drill sergeant Bob Service" who wants to convert a group of "liberal philosophers" into "goose-stepping Prussians." I have argued with him again and again, but he only laughs at me — or worse, promises me reforms that he has no intention of making.

I never make the mistake, as he does, of neglecting my relations with my partners, even the youngest. The associates I can afford to treat impersonally, with simple good manners, as it is never too late to cultivate the small number of them who will eventually be made members of the firm. Indeed, there may even be an advantage in the sudden offer of intimacy by the senior partner who has, until one's day of grace, seemed a remote figure. But with the actual partners I cultivate a near intimacy, taking them regularly to lunch, one by one, and inquiring into their problems, legal and domestic. I am counting on this to stand me in good stead in any showdown with Deane.

That such a showdown is on its way seems inevitable after what occurred at our first formal office dinner. We had taken a private dining room at the University Club for a party that included all partners and associates, together with their spouses or guests. Alice, you may be surprised to hear, was my "spouse" for the occasion.

She and I have been on much more friendly terms of late. On two occasions we have taken the girls out to Keswick for Sunday lunch, once with my parents and once with hers, and we have occasionally walked in the park with them on Saturday afternoons. Ours has become what is called a "civilized" separation, which means, I trust, that it will eventually end — at least when Alice comes to her senses. She has even helped with the arrangements for the office party, ordering the menu and the flowers and seating the dinner tables.

Her kindness, however, had to be used for her husband's benefit that night, for Deane, who had had, as usual, too many drinks, poked odious fun at my speech. I had tried to sound a serious note:

"A party like this should be a fun occasion, of course, but there's no law that says we cease to be good fellows if we have a moment of seriousness. So bear with me while I say this. We are a young firm. Our oldest lawyer is only thirty-seven. We haven't the 'advantage' of bad portraits of bearded forebears or medallions over the drinking fountains offering us samples of the wisdom of the past. But for that very reason we should remind ourselves from time to time that we are still parts of a great tradition. I have spoken to many of you about the hypocrisy of some older members of the bar who orate about public service as they pocket big fees, but that needn't mean that public service doesn't exist or that we can't be a part of it. I intend that we shall do our part in *pro bono* work. I expect us all to live up to the ideals we have inherited."

"Fortunately, we don't pay taxes on that kind of inheritance!"

Enough had been drunk so that even the more discreet associates laughed at Deane's barked interjection.

"All laughing aside," I retorted in a dry tone that partially restored the silence of the chamber, "I think it is necessary to recall these things, banal as it may sound. For we should be an instrument of justice as well as the servant of those who retain us, officers of the bar as well as spokesmen for business. The greatest law firms of this city stand for more than the roster of their clients, and I'll be damned if I don't live to see our firm become as great as any!"

"Our managing partner," Glenn now exclaimed, jumping to his feet amid the applause that followed my remarks, "has just seen fit to damn himself! For was it not precisely the turgid pomposity of the so-called great law firms that we pledged ourselves to break away from? And was it Bob Service, the lofty seeker of the eternal verities in the cerulean sky, whom we followed or the agile Bob who knew just when to place his dagger between the shoulder blades of Branders Blakelock?"

This, too, was greeted with some laughs, but they were nervous laughs. Everyone in that room could now feel that ours was no friendly argument.

"That's not a matter for levity!" I called out angrily.

"No, of course not. I crave your pardon for violating the Robert Service law of gravity!"

Alice after dinner came over to me and hooked her arm under mine to lead me away from the others.

"What an utter bastard Glenn is," she murmured in my ear. "Poor Bob, you were trying so hard. Maybe a bit too hard."

I was sore and angry that it should be so obvious that I needed sympathy, but it was still something to have Alice on my side. There was a feeling in her tone that made me want to ask why I should care what anyone thought about anything so long as she was with me.

"How about lunching with me tomorrow?" I asked her. "Do you realize you've never even seen my new offices?"

"I think I'd like that, Bob. Yes, I think I really would."

Now that it is beginning to look as if Alice might be thinking of coming back to me, I find myself a bit cooler in assessing her character. It is not that I don't want her back; I do. But I must be consistent with my long-held resolution of seeing things straight.

Alice is a wonderful woman, perhaps even a great one. She is large of spirit, generous and fine. Wherever you tap her with your hammer she rings true. My parents, who are also to some extent "true blues," though made of coarser material, instinctively appreciate her and take her side against their own child. But the essential difference between her and me is not that I am less

pure, less "good" than she — although I might be willing
to concede this — but that she will not recognize in her
own nature the spots and warts that I admit, however
reluctantly, in my own.

If "good people" are those who think they are good
and "bad people" are those who know they are bad, then
the election between souls that are saved and souls that
are damned becomes as arbitrary as any conceived by the
Jansenists of old. There is no real reason that with better
"public relations" I should not appear as noble a character as Alice.

For could I not have shown up Glenn Deane as motivated by near lunatic jealousy of my success? And
wasn't he? And could I not have presented Branders
Blakelock as a Dracula who sucks the life blood of
handsome young clerks? And isn't he? And might I not
have won Alice back by falling on my knees before her,
like Richard of York, and declaring that I had eviscerated
my old firm for her sake? And, in a way, hadn't I? Who
would benefit more than she by my greater revenues?

At Columbia I wrote a term paper on the novels of
Dame Ivy Compton-Burnett. That marvelous old maid
conceived of humanity as divided into sheep and goats,
the former a submissive passive majority and the latter a
shrill dominating minority. The sheep have only their
wit and irony with which to resist the tyranny of the
latter, but this sometimes suffices, as the pompous goats
are extremely sensitive to ridicule. What I learned from
Dame Ivy is that human beings may be milder and more
tepid than their supposed counterparts in heroic fiction

and drama, and that, like the lower animals, they run truer to type than idealists suppose. If I am to be a goat, I must not allow the barbs of the silly sheep to destroy me.

Yet Alice, sitting before the desk in my new office the next day, before we went to lunch, seemed quite unprepared with barbs. She was unstinting in her praise of my pale yellow walls, my emerald-green carpet, my eight large flower prints.

"They're Thorntons, aren't they?"

Indeed they were. I was surprised at her perspicacity, but when pictures had a literary flavor she was apt to be on target. I loved these romantic prints. The corollas of the flowers were huge and brilliant, like the heads of beautiful, dangerous women, and the landscapes were distant panoramas, adapted to the supposed moods of the plants. A poisonous arum was seen before a rainstorm breaking over gray, craggy peaks, roses grew before the backdrop of a ruined temple, some eighteenth-century *folie*, and the night-blooming cereus exploded as in fire before a Gothic church outlined in the moonlight. What was I but a humble mortal before the glorious carnivorous plant of the law? Behind my desk I had hung the sacred Egyptian lotus, an explosion of golden petals dominating a distant dim desert where small pyramids, symbols of death, were arranged.

"You may ask why I put flowers in a law office," I said. "It's because they are my idea of what is at once civilized and savage."

"Let's go to lunch, Bob."

"Do you mind if I talk for a minute about my philosophy of law? You've never really believed that I had one."

"Right now?"

"Yes. Because I want you to hear it before I formally propose that we come back together again."

Alice gave me a long look in which I thought I could read several things. But I think that assent — or at least a willingness to consider assent — was one of them. Or was she simply debating that for the girls' sake, and my sake, or perhaps even for her own, she had better make the best of me? That I was a bit mad, but perhaps not as wicked as she had neurotically assumed?

"I'm listening, Bob."

I told her now, in all gravity, that I was determined that my firm should be a success. And not just a financial success, either: a *moral* success. I was resolved that it would be a union of highly trained, competent men and women who would do everything for a client that could be lawfully done. We should be taut, keen, hard-boiled, comprehensive. There would be no room for sentimentality and none for sloppiness. Uniform rules of office procedure would be laid down and rigidly adhered to; overhead would be kept strictly under control. Partners and associates would be paid in accordance with the quality of their labor and the fees that it produced. The perfect machinery of the firm would be totally at the service of its legal expertise.

And what would that expertise be used for? Well, first and foremost, of course, for the clients — for the skillful handling of their interests within the last letter of the law, but never a millimeter beyond. Nor would the client ever be subjected to the smallest piece of moral advice or guidance; all such matters would be strictly the client's affair. My firm would be a sharp cutting weapon to be picked up and used; weapons did not preach, but they had to be paid for. On the other hand, when we operated in the public area — and I was willing to commit us to a substantial number of hours a week for *pro bono* work — then we would show an equal zeal and an equal ruthlessness. Even should my biggest client, for example, Atlantic Rylands, object to a suit that we were bringing — say, on an environmental issue — it would be told, politely but firmly, to mind its own business.

When I had finished Alice was silent. Then she asked unexpectedly, "Do you ever see Mr. Blakelock? I wonder what he'd think of your ideals?"

"As a matter of fact I had lunch with him last week. I told him just what I've told you."

"And what did he say?"

I hesitated for several moments. But then I saw, in what I deemed a flash of true Service inspiration, that the truth was precisely what might clinch her coming back to me. "He wasn't very nice. He said that what I was really doing was putting together a firm that another Robert Service would not be able to eviscerate."

Alice's hands flew to her mouth in a gesture of combined horror and amusement. "Ah, the wicked man!" she cried. Then she got up. "Let's go to lunch, darling." Darling? I was right! "I'm starved. But don't worry; I'm on your side. I shan't be a silly ass again. At least not for a while, I hope. Oh, Bob, the world takes a lot of knowing, doesn't it?"

One thing I resolved, when I returned to work after our long and happy meal in which we split a bottle of Pouilly-Fumé, was to continue to keep this journal in my office after I should have come home to my old apartment. I have no intention of taking the chance that Alice might read of my intention somehow to dispose of Glenn Deane. She has not yet learned to accept the necessity of getting rid of rotten apples or the fact that the "good life" is only bought at a price. But I am now fairly confident that Alice can learn this in time. After all, she is very intelligent.

I have told Douglas Hyde to keep a sharp eye on Deane. Douglas is my "number two" in the firm, my "executive officer," a large-featured, snowy-haired young man who never loses his temper, a silent operator who sees that life is funny without more than smirking at it, an indefatigable worker and, I guess, as ambitious a lawyer as myself. Douglas would use me, but it would be for my benefit as well as his own. He and I are a team.

·⑨·

WELL, I HAVE "done the deed."

For Glenn at last was guilty of something gravely out of line with the policy of our firm. At a meeting in my office of the executive committee, consisting of him, myself, Douglas Hyde and Peter Stubbs, he actually suggested that three of "his" associates, because of the "splendid" work they had done for his client Ace Investors, be given an extra award of five thousand dollars apiece despite the fact that the Christmas bonuses to the lawyers and staff had already been announced.

"But that's preposterous!" I exclaimed. "It would throw our whole compensation scheme out of whack. What can you be thinking of, Glenn?"

"I'm thinking of three crack lawyers who have worked their asses off and deserve to be rewarded for their missing posteriors."

"All our people work hard."

"Not like mine, kiddo. Not like mine."

"That's ridiculous! And even if it were so, it's no reason to make invidious distinctions. We can't run a firm if every partner is going to demand special treatment for his associates."

"Every partner? Am I every partner?"

"All right, any partner."

"That's hogwash, Bob, and you know it. The partners who bring in the bacon are entitled to have their minor requests honored without all this haggling. Hell, I'd vote the same bonus for your people."

"But I'd never ask it. That's the difference between us. This business of firms within firms has got to stop. This business of partners acting as lobbyists for their own departments. Quit being such a mother hen, Glenn! Your chicks are no more yours than they are Peter's or Doug's or mine."

Now why did I have to be quite so nasty? Was I spoiling for a fight? I was. I had the feeling that a showdown was due between us and that it was better to push it while I held the good cards.

Glenn, I should explain, now seemed to me the very embodiment of all that was wrong with our world. He was violent and undisciplined. He grabbed whatever it pleased him to grab. And having no morals, or even any guiding principles, he protected himself in the only way such a creature could — with a bodyguard of unquestioning dependents. Wasn't that the way all civilizations were fated to end, with Alarics and Attilas leading troops of blindly loyal ruffians into bloody and ruthless battle against each other? Where the loyalty of the lesser to the greater brute was the only quality left that could even be said to resemble a virtue?

Glenn, at any rate, called for a vote, although, as a committee, we had always acted on consensus. When he lost, three to one, he announced furiously that he would take the matter to the firm, which he proceeded to do at the next of our biweekly lunches.

These lunches, which were faithfully attended by every partner not actually in court or at a closing or out of town, were held in a private dining room in a midtown lunch club. After a first course of general chatter, I would call the meeting to order and initiate the discussion of firm matters. It was then that I responded to Glenn's demand for the three bonuses denied by the committee:

"Let me say at once, gentlemen, that I regard the question of compensation as within the exclusive jurisdiction of the executive committee. That committee cannot be reversed. It can only be abolished and a new committee appointed in its place. A vote in favor of Mr. Deane's resolution is in effect a vote to abolish the committee."

"I don't give a damn how I get my bonuses," Glenn retorted in his most grating tone, "so long as I get them. If abolishing the executive committee is the only efficient way to run this firm, then I say let's abolish it!" He glared defiantly around the table. "And, yes, I *do* so move. Are you going to second my motion, Lew?"

"I second it, Glenn."

"Address the chair, please!" I called out.

"I second it, Mr. Service." Lew Pessen was Glenn's particular sidekick.

"Very well, the motion is made and seconded," I announced tartly. "Before it is voted on I ask every partner to consider carefully the effect of this procedure on the future of the firm. You will be deciding whether you wish to be managed by rules or by whim. You will be deciding whether every policy of your chosen managers will be subject to reversal by any disgruntled partner who shouts for special treatment."

"Can't we just vote on a simple bonus question without all this emotion?" cried Glenn.

"I want to finish, Mr. Deane. I want to emphasize the extreme gravity of this vote on the welfare of the firm." I paused here for several seconds. "Very well, will all those in favor of the motion please raise their right hand."

Three hands in addition to Glenn's were promptly raised. The motion was lost. But four was a dangerous dissent. I resolved that the war with Deane should now be to the death. As he was volatile and I was patient it should not be too long before I found the proper time and cause.

And indeed my opportunity came sooner than I expected. Only a week after the turbulent partners' lunch meeting, in a discussion with Douglas Hyde about the firm's reaction to our now distributed Christmas bonuses, I made an important discovery. The reaction had been unanimously enthusiastic.

"Even with Deane's disappointed trio?" I asked sharply.

"Even them. They don't seem disappointed at all. In fact, I hear they seem particularly smug about something."

I jumped up from my desk. "That's it, then!" I cried. I was too excited for a second to say more.

"What's *it*?" he demanded.

"They've been paid their five g's!"

"You mean Glenn paid their bonuses out of his own pocket?"

"No, no, he'd never do that. Glenn fork over fifteen thousand bucks? Dream on. Ace Investors must have paid it."

"Because they're so happy with our legal services they'll pay bonuses to our associates?"

"Hardly. They would have taken it out of our fee."

"How could they do that?"

"Very simply. By reducing our bill by that amount."

"But we'd have known!"

"Not unless Glenn chose to tell us. Don't be dense, Doug."

"Oh, I see what you're getting at. Glenn cut the firm's bill by fifteen grand and asked the client to pay his three associates directly."

"Exactly. Ace Investors would have regarded it as irregular, but Glenn must have insisted that it was important for his three clerks' morale to feel the direct appreciation of the client. And, of course, he would have guaranteed the firm's approval. So they went along. Glenn Deane robbed his partners to pay his pets!"

"How do we prove it?"

"I suggest you call one of your pals at Ace Investors,

Doug. Tell him you have a bookkeeping problem. Ask him if the payments to the three associates were for five g's or twenty-five hundred."

"Won't he be suspicious?"

"Why? Won't Glenn have told him the firm approved the payments?"

Thus I discovered that the payments had actually been made. There was no time to lose. Douglas confirmed my suspicions on a Monday; the morrow was the day of our next partners' lunch. I even wondered if I dared wait so many hours. Should I call the firm into special session in the conference room that very afternoon? If Glenn found out that I knew, he would have the chance to go to the partners, one by one, and plead his case. I should have lost the needed elements of surprise and shock.

But even as I debated my course of action he came to see me. I could always tell when Glenn knew he was in trouble; his oiliness became almost unbearable. It was as if, with his general contempt for the world around him, he wanted to satisfy himself that he could prevail over his opponent's worst opinion of him. "You think I'm a hypocrite," he would seem to be saying. "Well, damn right I'm a hypocrite! And a brilliant hypocrite like me can overcome an ass like you with all his cards face up on the table!"

"We haven't been seeing much of each other lately, Bob," he began with a kind of leer. "I don't know why that should be. After all, we're really the daddy and mummy of this firm, aren't we?"

"Which of us is the daddy?"

"Oh, you are, dear boy, you are. With my big paps and ass I might be an old milking mater, mightn't I? When are we going to lunch?"

"How about Wednesday?"

"You're on, kid. And by the way, if you should come across any little irregularity in the compensation of my associates, don't get too excited. If it's laid at my door, I can always make adjustments. Even, if absolutely essential, at my own expense."

"What sort of irregularities do you have in mind?"

"Mere details, my friend, mere details. We can talk about it on Wednesday."

I breathed a sigh of relief as he left my office. He actually trusted me to wait! Surely this was a sign of weakness. I looked forward now to what I should do the next day. Why not? I had suffered enough humiliation from Glenn. I had offered him chance after chance. Now I should simply destroy him. And enjoy it!

At the partners' lunch on Tuesday I waited until the usual time for the discussion of business. Then I rose.

"I have an announcement of the utmost importance to make," I called down the table. An ominous silence fell. "Following which, I must ask for the resignation of a partner. If that partner chooses not to resign, I shall move that we dissolve the firm and re-form it without him. If the firm rejects my solution, I shall submit my own resignation."

"Who the shit do you think you are?" Glenn shouted at me. He had had more than one of the cocktails that we served before the meal. "Is this Bobby Service I see before me, or Robespierre demanding the head of Danton from the Committee of Public Safety?"

"You have only to listen, Glenn," I retorted coolly, "and then judge for yourself. It is indeed your resignation that I am asking for. I submit that you reduced a bill to Ace Investors by fifteen thousand dollars on the understanding that it would issue checks of five thousand each to three associates designated by you. And I don't have to tell anyone in this room who those three associates were."

"I deny it absolutely!"

"Do you think I haven't checked it out with your client? I'm not crazy, Mr. Deane."

"Are you all going to sit here and put up with this?" Glenn almost screamed. "Take down your pants, Service, and let them kiss your ass!"

A burst of questions now hit me.

"What the hell's going on here?"

"What were the checks for?"

"Why were you spying on Glenn?"

"Gentlemen, gentlemen!" I called. "The matter is a simple one. Glenn Deane made the unilateral decision that the compensation of three of his associates was inadequate. He requested special bonuses for them, which were refused by the executive committee on the ground that they would throw our compensation system out of balance and create firm-wide jealousy and dissatisfaction. Mr. Deane thereupon proceeded to take our management into his own hands. He reduced a firm bill to a client on the understanding that the client would issue checks totaling the sum reduced directly to the three lawyers involved. Do you still deny it, Mr. Deane?"

"I won't answer, you shithead."

"Mr. Deane," I continued, addressing the table in cold triumph, "has diverted firm funds for his private purposes. It is embezzlement, pure and simple. I don't know about the rest of you, but I do not propose to continue practicing law in the same firm with a man who has behaved in this fashion."

There was a great deal of shouting and screaming after this, and it was ultimately agreed that the partners should be given more time to think it over. The next week was a hectic one in which I was constantly visited by groups with different offers of compromise. Deane, I was assured, would never do such a thing again. Deane would gladly return the fifteen thousand dollars to the firm. Deane would agree to resign from the executive committee and interfere no more with my control of the firm.

But I was adamant. I knew that he could never be trusted. I assured each partner that I would never practice law with him again. And they knew that I meant it; that was the great thing. They knew that I would walk out of the firm alone, if necessary, and take a vital part of its business with me. Furthermore, even to those who regarded me as harsh and autocratic there was no disgrace in siding with me. Glenn Deane had defrauded them; I never had. They might deplore my lack of mercy, my absence of charity, but they had to concede that I was only living up to my often enunciated principles.

In the end Glenn resigned and went to work for Ace Investors. Only one partner, Lew Pessen, left with him. And we kept Ace as a client! I was perfectly aware that my rule would be resented for some time to come. But it had been established; that was the real point. I could afford to be lenient now, at least until I had patched together our broken unity. I had done the only thing I could have done. I realized it, and I slept well of nights.

And now I come to the shattering aftermath. Lynne Deane went to see Alice in her office and called me every name in the book. When Alice and I next met, I was informed by my now marble-faced, alienated wife that the question of our reconciliation was closed.

· 10 ·

"I SHOULD HAVE THOUGHT Lynne's abuse might
have recommended me to you," I protested to Alice.
"She was never a favorite of yours."

"But you don't deny that you threw Glenn out of the
firm?"

Patiently, if a bit wearily, I recounted the facts.

"And you wouldn't give him a second chance?"

"Of course not. The whole point was to be rid of him.
It was a golden opportunity. He might have been too
smart ever to give me another."

"Oh, my God, you plotted it! Oh, Robert, Robert,
can't you see what's happening to you?"

"How can a man not become whatever it is you think
I'm becoming when his wife leaves him for doing his
job?"

"Then you *do* see it?"

"I see what you think you see." I turned away from
her with despair in my heart. "But I'm tired of your

illusions, Alice! You think you're like Scrooge's girl friend in *A Christmas Carol*, who gives him up because she feels his heart is turning to gold. So noble, so sad, so firm. But what horse manure it all is! My work supports a hundred people. Before I'm through it may be five times that number. And all you can see is that I've taken off my gloves to handle an s.o.b. the only way he can be handled! All right, let's give up on reconciliation. What more can I say?"

What I had to despair of ever making Alice see was that I was not immoral. I simply accepted the basic greed and selfishness of human beings. I recognized that they are always going to act in their own interests and that they should be allowed to do so except where an actual crime to person or property was threatened. To avoid crime in law was the sole moral imperative, and it was imposed on man not by God but by man. Yet on that sole imperative hung all "the law and the prophets." A man could go right up to the threshold of crime, but not a step farther. Not even a half step! Alice, for the life of her, couldn't see this as a moral code. But to me it is the only valid one. The rest is cant.

My dissent from Alice's code may spring from a dichotomy between myself and the culture in which we were both raised, a dichotomy that was probably the determining cause for the form my personality has taken. For I could never see that there was any real substance to the idols that my elders respected or purported to respect. They were not only hollow, but you could *see* they were hollow, or if you had any doubt about it, you had only to give one of them a tap.

It was not only my father's false pride in his lowly position in his law firm that had disgusted me. That had simply provided a start to my speculations. I could also see that the congregation in the church where he passed the plate was either daydreaming or wrestling with dark doubts. None of them, I was convinced, believed in the efficacy of their orisons or in an afterlife. Indeed, the church had fallen to such low esteem that some of my family's friends half apologized for attending services, explaining that they enjoyed the "poetry" of the old ritual. To avoid the bald terror of the idea of extinction I suppose they clutched at a wild hope of some kind of survival, however nebulous, and then firmly turned their thoughts from it. And Protestants not only don't believe in the virgin birth, they tend to regard their ministers as namby-pambies. A "real" man would go in for success, wouldn't he, and success is power, and what is power, as the Bible puts it, but being able to say to this man, Go, and he goeth, and to that man, Come, and he cometh? And what of the multitudinous majority that can never come to power? Oh, they have "dignity" or "honor," like my old man.

Even in their personal lives the grinning idols rang false. The "love" of which they prated, as the be-all and end-all of life, was either a mild sentimentality or a mere sexual impulse. Parental duty was the artificial continuation of an instinct; a child's duty to a parent was a myth. What made me bitter was not so much the real world, which was understandable and could be coped with, but the thing that people made of it, a bedizened and tinseled Christmas tree as opposed to a noble fir standing proud in the forest. When I hid my thoughts from the world, I found that my blond and blue-eyed boyish looks made a perfect mask. I have always at least looked the fool that so many people try conscientiously to be.

But the great thing about Alice was that from the beginning of our friendship at the age of sixteen I never associated her with any of the falseness of our suburban community. She was at all times, as she still is, totally and sublimely honest. She may have believed in the idols, but they never made *her* hollow. Wherever I put my hammer on her soul it rang loud and true. And as I write this it breaks my heart to face the fact that I have lost her.

We were in love through all of our four years at Columbia, and it was not until we were seniors that she began to be troubled about me. I think that one of the reasons that she was so late in conceiving her doubts was her intense gratitude to me for accepting her scruples about sexual intercourse. Many, perhaps most of our classmates, children of the sexual revolution, immediately converted their casual attractions to affairs, but Alice belonged to the minority of women who believed in preserving their virginity until marriage. She did not criticize those of more liberal views; she simply insisted that she had to be true to what she believed was right for herself.

"I do not want to belong to you until I know I shall belong to you for life," she would solemnly tell me.

I was so much in love that I was grateful to settle for her not going out with other men. So long as I could be sure of being the exclusive object of her affections I was able to put up with almost anything. There were times, I confess, when even the knowledge that I was wholly loved by the glowing creature at my side did not guarantee my fidelity, but Alice never knew of any falling off, or if she did, she was big enough to look the other way, allowing me the latitude of our era. But nothing of any real emotional importance occurred to me in all that time aside from Alice.

Her doubts arose over some of my opinions rather than over anything that I actually did. It distressed her that I was reluctant to go "all out" on issues over which she, like most college students of the time, felt passionately, as for example, when I defended American opposition to communism in Vietnam or suggested that Richard Nixon's brand of patriotism was not wholly contemptible. But what was worse than any particular difference of opinion between us was Alice's growing suspicion that there was apt to be a reservation on my part behind our apparent accord: that I tended to believe that most proposed social cures were as bad as or worse than the disease they purported to treat, that idealists were usually talking through their hats and that two opinions always existed as to the degree of any villain's iniquity.

"I never seem to be able to tie you down," she would complain.

"Why should you want to?" I would retort. "Can't you live and let live?"

But she couldn't. She was disturbed by my tolerance

of opinions that she found obnoxious. She didn't, for example, think it was at all funny when I quipped: "Some of my best friends are anti-Semites," and she wouldn't go out with me for a week when I refused to sign a petition calling for an investigation of police brutality. Alice could be very stern indeed.

But our greatest difficulty came over her father. Alice adored Jock Norton with a hero worship that made the faintest implied criticism of him seem a besmirching mud attack, and her suspicions of my habit of mental reservation made it hard for me to be convincingly enthusiastic. Besides, I didn't like Norton. It is always difficult to like someone who dislikes oneself, and Alice's father was always sniffing out the philistine that he obviously believed to be lurking under my exterior of good will.

Norton was a man of studied amiability and sly sarcasms who would keep you under relentless oral examination until you began to sense how much hostility might underlie that probing curiosity. For years he had been in the habit of offering me exaggerated compliments with only the faintest note of mockery: compliments on my looks, my athletic aptitude, my popularity, my good marks, my interest in literature. But when, as undergraduates at Columbia, Alice and I began to go steady, a more acerb note crept into his treatment of me. He would keep his glinting eyes fixed on me as if I were some interesting freak, running his long fingers through his long greasy hair, chewing the ends of his glasses, twisting his thin restless body as if to defy me to define his undeniable charm, as he said such things as:

"I never cease to marvel, dear boy, at your spirited enthusiasm for such florid decadents as Walter Pater and John Addington Symonds. That a young man who might play Stover in a film version of 'Stover at Yale' should interest himself in the lacquered prose of those two old queens bespeaks wonders for the tolerance of your generation."

"But if I could write, Mr. Norton, I should like to write like Pater."

"Ah, the bleak wind that blows from the pure hills of youth! Avast, ye spirits of the glorious dead who made fetishes of the pungent phrase, the club that was called a club, the Anglo-Saxon term, the four-letter word! Shades of Hemingway and O'Hara, begone! Henry James is god, and Pater is his prophet!"

"Is it necessary to choose between writers? Can't we keep them all?"

At this moment Norton became almost serious. "No! Nobody ever loved literature who loved it all! Of course we must choose!"

I had the distinct feeling that Norton disliked the idea of anything sexual between me and his daughter, not so much because he wanted to keep her, in a Freudian sense, for himself, as because he did not want her to give pleasure to any man. He was jealous, really, not so much of me as of her. I am quite sure that I am not making up this homosexual side of Norton's nature. It was the only thing that really explained his hostility. So long as he could not have me for himself — and I believe he was not a practicing but an inhibited pederast — he did not want anyone — certainly not a woman, most of all his beloved daughter — to have me. Norton was drawn to good-looking young men, but he hated them for the very attraction that they exercised, and he did all he could to make them seem boobs in contrast to his brilliant self. Oh, they might have beautiful bodies, yes — much good it would do them! — but who had a mind as beautiful and a wit as sharp as Jock Norton?

Of course, he always pretended friendship for me. He would even, on occasion, ask me to join him for dinner, just the two of us, at the Yale Club, where he always drank a good deal too much. Like the Baron de Charlus in Proust's novel he could not resist the subject of homosexuality, but being of a later generation he did not have to pretend to scorn it. On the contrary, he maintained an attitude of lofty, detached tolerance.

On one of these occasions he drank so much that I believe he was actually on the verge of betraying himself, not only to me but to himself. An evening headline about a march to promote gay rights gave him the start that he needed on a favorite subject.

"Your friends have no prejudices in that field, do they, Bob?"

"It depends what you call a prejudice. Some of us regard inversion as an aberration. However, we certainly don't think one should persecute aberrations. But most gays think that even calling them ill shows prejudice."

"And you think that's what they are?"

"Sick? Yes. And most sick people are curable. Particularly if you catch them early enough."

"So at the first hint in your infant son of such depravity — say, that you observe him admiring a butterfly or showing no interest in peeking under his baby sister's skirt — you'd whisk him off to the nearest manly shrink?"

"To answer the question behind the persiflage — yes, essentially, I would."

"You don't think that in placing psychological blinkers on his young eyes and heading him towards the 'quivering thigh' and parts adjacent of a female of the species, you might have blunted sensitivities perhaps indispensable to the development of an artist?"

"I suppose I'd have to take that chance. But do you assume that Proust would have become a doctor like his father and brother had he not been a fag?"

"Oh, I assume nothing. I leave assumptions to youth. I should not even assume that there is such a thing as a fag, as you call it."

"What do you call it?"

"Nothing. A man committing a homosexual act, in my opinion, is not a homosexual. He is simply a man committing a homosexual act. I wonder how many men have never been guilty of one — or of wanting to be guilty of one."

"I haven't."

"You, my dear fellow? With your love of Pater and Symonds? You disappoint me. I shouldn't have thought you so crude!"

What did his long serious stare mean? Was Alice's father actually going to make a pass? Something like panic crept over me. Suppose she were to find out that her old man was her rival? Would I not forever be hopelessly identified with the nausea that such a discovery would bring about? I had to put an end to it in some way that would warn him before he fatally exposed himself.

"Do you really think, Mr. Norton, that I could ever look your daughter in the face again if I had such filthy thoughts? Come now. Admit you're just being a cautious parent and testing me."

Norton seemed confused by this, but he abandoned the odious subject and soon left me to go up alone to his room, where he presumably dropped into an inebriated slumber. At any rate he never brought up the topic with me again, and it was noticeable that for some months thereafter he cut down on his drinking. I think he had had a bad scare.

Certainly he never forgave me, and his revenge took a peculiarly ugly form. In one of his short stories, which appeared in *Good Housekeeping*, he drew a savage caricature of me in the person of one Uriel Heemuth (designed, of course, to suggest Dickens's villain), a student at Harvard who cultivates all the socially important men of his class, but always with an avowedly unworldly motive, as Mr. Rich Kid because he plays the piano, or Mr. High Society because he writes poetry for the *Advocate*. Uriel Heemuth is ultimately seen through and rejected, and in a fit of repentance and self-disgust he goes to call on an old, sick, retired professor of philosophy in Cambridge, a friend of his father's whom he has been urged to look up but whom until now he has not deemed important enough to be worth it. Of course, there he finds, gathered respectfully around the old sage, all the cream of the class. The shunned philosopher has become his social open sesame! Moral: a determined enough climber will always make it, one way or another.

And how did I know that Uriel Heemuth was Robert Service? Very simply. Not only did the physical description of the character match me perfectly, but he was represented as an enthusiast of such "purple prose" writers as Symonds and Pater, though only with a view to drape his own social and material ambitions in the garb of a cultivated littérateur. It was a real hatchet job.

And there was no way that I could even hint to Alice the nature of my suspicions as to the origin of her father's animosity. If I should have done so and convinced her, she might have been dangerously depressed. And if I had failed to convince her, I should have dished myself forever in her good graces. All I could do was take the whole business as a kind of joke on her father's part. But this did not keep her from being very upset, particularly when her father took the lofty position that there was no reference intended to me and refused to discuss the matter.

It was her mother, Isabel, who finally put an end to our difficulty and in a most unexpected manner. She was a bright, jumpy, twittering little bird of a woman who ordinarily played a secondary role in the lives of her more brilliant husband and daughter, but who could be surprisingly assertive if the occasion required. This was such an occasion. Her husband was away on a fishing trip, and Alice and I were spending a Saturday night in Keswick in our respective homes. I had gone over to the Nortons' for supper.

"I don't want to hear another word about that wretched short story," Isabel snapped, the moment Alice, inevitably, referred to it. "It's the meanest thing I ever heard of. Now you listen to me, Alice. And you, too, Bob. Jock Norton all his life has been a poseur. He wants to blame someone else for the fact that he's not Ernest Hemingway or F. Scott Fitzgerald. And I happen to be a very handy person to blame. It's my tastes, my extravagance, my middle-class values that have chained him down, turned him into a hack writer of potboilers, a money-making machine. All right. I'll go along. I'm perfectly willing to be the fall guy. Let him have his fantasies if they make him happy. But when he spreads them over into your lives, when he identifies himself with you, Alice, and picks on Bob here to be your excuse — in advance — in case you one day fail to be Virginia Woolf or Katherine Anne Porter or whoever else he happens to have in mind, then I cry: 'Cut it out! That won't do, Buster!' Bob is as fine a young man as I know, and I'm not going to stand for your father mussing up your life because of some neurotic illusions of his own. Let him keep them to himself!"

Alice, pale and grave, must have stared at her mother for five seconds of shocked surprise. Then, to my astonishment and joy, she got up, came over to my chair and leaned down to kiss me on the lips.

"Oh, Bob, darling, I'm so sorry!"

And then she burst into tears.

Later that night, after her mother had retired, we decided to marry immediately after graduation. We had talked before of waiting until I had finished law school, but now she insisted that she wanted to belong to me entirely and would go to work to help support us until I was qualified to practice. It was certainly the happiest day of my life.

And certainly the three years at Columbia Law School were the happiest of our married life. Alice and I seemed to have no conflicts then. She worked in a publishing house and loved it, and I made the discovery that I was just as fascinated by the law as I ever had been by letters. Was there, after all, so very much difference? In our discussions of law and life and literature Alice and I seemed at last in pleasant accord. If there were times when it occurred to me that she was flying a bit too high above our terrestrial abode — that it might not be feasible, when the day came that would call upon me to earn my living, to put all her ideals into daily practice — she was still as necessary to me as the shining, glorious sun is to the weeds that push sturdily up from the soil below. Robert Browning, inspired by Plato, spoke of the broken arcs on earth, the perfect round in heaven. The fact that my arcs were broken did not mean that I could not worship Alice's distant perfection.

And have I really lost all that? It seems so.

· 11 ·

I HAD, of course, to adjust myself to my now confirmed loneliness. I should have to equip myself, not only with new friends, but with something of a new philosophy to guide me in the path into which I had been thrust. Like Marius of Pater's beautiful novel, in the golden Rome of the Antonines, I should have to keep sampling theories of life, with eyes wide open to find some pattern in seeming chaos. And I was also going to need a girl friend. Misery would not make me a monk.

For a considerable time now my evenings had been divided between work at the office and reading in my room at the Stafford. I had become so absorbed in the firm that I did not seem to need any interest other than my faithful classics and an occasional movie. But I came to realize that some kind of a social life was indispensable to the managing partner of a firm that was long on talent and short on personal connections, and of course there were the demands of sex. As I had always detested the idea of purchased love and thought it unwise to get involved with women in the office, whether lawyers or staff, it behooved me to look about.

Actually, it was through the office that I met Sylvia Sands, and through her that I reorganized both my social and sex lives. So you might say that I killed two birds with one stone. Not that Sylvia was a stone — far from it.

Al Cornelius, president of Atlantic Rylands, had taken a great liking to me and often wanted me with him, even on occasions where legal advice was not strictly necessary. He was a grim, silent, self-made man, astonishingly lean and youthful at fifty, with close-cropped thick gray hair, who was constantly analyzing people and their problems and coming up with terse, gruff, cynical and usually accurate appraisals. He had taken on the chairmanship of the board of the Colonial Museum, one of the cultural institutions enshrined behind white columns in the complex of buildings unhappily far north at 155th Street on the Hudson. The job had challenged Al because it seemed so hopeless. The collection was priceless; the endowment tiny; the public absent. I met him there one afternoon in the board room to discuss a fundraising program with a public relations expert. Two other trustees, members of the drive committee, were also present.

Mrs. Sands, the expert, was about my age, or even a touch older, a handsome blonde who spoke in a clear level tone with a very precise articulation.

"I suppose you're all aware that you're going to get most of your money from a few big donors in the early months of the campaign. Charity begins literally at home, and we'll start with the trustees. May I suggest an amount for you to pledge, Mr. Cornelius?"

"You may *suggest* anything you like, my dear lady."

"Could you see your way to pledging a hundred thousand dollars?"

"No way. I have too many commitments."

"I didn't say you had to pay it, of course. I said you should pledge it."

"Is that quite straight?"

"Perfectly straight. You pledge your 'best efforts' to raise it. That does not create a legal liability."

Cornelius turned to me. "Is that so, Bob?"

"Yes. That gives me no trouble, Al."

"But, Mrs. Sands," my client pursued, "mightn't people think I was legally committed?"

"Are we to be concerned about that?"

"Well, well. You *are* a cool customer."

"Put it this way, Mr. Cornelius. There are four members of your board who are too rich to be seen doing less than the chairman. They will give what he pledges. I have seen this happen again and again. A pledge from you will guarantee us a four hundred thousand dollar start."

"Very well, I'll pledge it. Just as you say. And who knows? I might even pay it."

I looked now with admiration at the cool Mrs. Sands. Her blonde hair was perfectly set. Everything about her was prepared, manicured, scrupulously shining and neat. Yet she could hardly have been a woman with hours to spend at her dressing table. She had to be as efficient in

her toilet as in her business. Her regular features, her
calm gray eyes, her air of stillness, enhanced my original
sense of her almost movie-star loveliness, yet on closer
inspection I could see that she was the least bit dry, a
too typical American blonde. And then, as she continued
to outline her fund-raising plans, the seriousness, even
the gravity, of her nature, corrected once more my mis-
impression. She seemed to be trying to look like what she
felt the well-dressed career woman as pictured in *Vogue*
or *Harper's Bazaar* had to look like. Yet she was probably
too smart to believe that she had wholly succeeded or
perhaps even to care. As I watched her look up from her
notes at each man as he questioned her, I took in her air
of total attention, which, nonetheless — and without
suggesting the least failure of good manners — did not
even attempt to conceal that it was a business mask.

"That is right, Mr. Seldon. We have to have a membership drive as well. Of course, we will not expect
much revenue from that. We can't charge more than
fifteen or twenty dollars a year, and a good sixty per
cent will not renew. But the foundations believe in
membership drives. Even if we take a loss on it, I'm
afraid it's indispensable."

"Is that true of the mail drive, too?"

"Well, it's what we call the widow's mite. It's not the
mite that counts, but how it affects your major contribu-
tors. Big donors hate to feel they're doing the whole
thing. The widow's mite makes them feel that the
burden's being shared."

"Even if it's not?"

"Well, they're apt to take the wish for the deed. There are certain rituals in these campaigns."

"But a mail drive like this one is a terrible waste of paper. What do we expect by way of response? Two per cent? Will all our national forests be consumed by these voluminous appeals?"

"If you have conservationists on your board who object to that, we might try to work out something by telephone. Or even a radio appeal. TV is best, of course, but I don't think we can afford it, unless a station will donate the time."

I was beginning to be fascinated. Did nothing daunt her? Had she no principles? Would she work simultaneously on pro- and anti-abortion programs? For the NAACP and South African investors? Would she undertake a campaign to rehabilitate the Mafia? The only hint I had that she was human was my sense that she knew I was watching her. Once I thought she sent me the trace of a smile, as if she recognized that I was "on" to her.

I was to see a lot more of Mrs. Sands that day, because after our conference my client drove directly home to Greenwich and suggested that I give our fund raiser a lift downtown in a cab. She had promised the director of the museum that she would first visit a loan show of old ecclesiastic treasures: chalices, reliquaries, ciboriums and the like, and I accompanied her to the large, dark, unpeopled central gallery.

She walked slowly but without stopping past the glass cases of glittering objects. We paused at last before a missal bound in silver gilt and studded with large semiprecious stones.

I broke our silence. "Doesn't it make you feel that God must have been an old Jewish banker living on Fifth Avenue behind a Beaux Arts front?"

Again her faint smile seemed to confirm our sympathy. "Well, J. P. Morgan went in for this kind of thing, too. But he lived in a brownstone on Madison."

"When he ran his fingertips over those stones, do you suppose he thought of God?"

"As you imply, *his* god."

"A god who likes the bones and teeth and nails of his saints immured in gold and studded with opals!"

"Is your god so different, Mr. Service?"

"Do you ask that because I'm a lawyer?"

"Let's just say I ask it."

"I don't suppose I really have a god. Have you?"

"I'm perfectly prepared to have any god who can convince me he is one."

"But he hasn't so far?"

She didn't answer me, but continued her tour of the cases.

On the way downtown in the taxi we became more personal. She told me that she was a widow and lived with her ten-year-old son in an apartment on East Ninety-fourth Street. I informed her in turn of the state of my marriage. When we arrived at her house, she paused for a moment before getting out, apparently considering something. Then, with her hand on the door she said abruptly:

"I'm dining tonight with a friend of mine, Ethelinda

Low. Perhaps you've heard of her? She's a kind of Mrs. New York. She always lets me bring a man. Would you care to come?"

"I'd like to very much."

"Good. Pick me up at eight. Black tie."

She told me about our hostess later, in the cab on our way to the party. Mrs. Low, like Odette in *Swann*, of obscure, indeed, unfathomable social origin, had started her career more or less as a kept woman and then had married, first, a restaurateur, second, a Brooklyn contractor, and finally, twice widowed, old Sidney Low of railroad fame. She was a woman of colossal energy who had brought to the management of the great fortune that her third husband had bequeathed outright to her a mind, in someone's phrase, "unclouded by the usual American fetishes about the spending of money acquired by sweat, will or altar." According to Sylvia, she had earned the total respect and even admiration of New York society.

We found our hostess standing by the doorway of her living room, formally receiving her guests. Gray-haired and brown-skinned, but very tall and straight and endowed with the most serene blue eyes I had ever seen, Mrs. Low in no way suggested her beginnings. She had converted such youthful spirits as might have been needed in earlier days to an almost awesome respectability. Yet at the same time she impressed me as a person who had no desire to appear as anything than what she evidently now was: a wise, rich, sensible, down-to-earth woman. I was later to learn that all of her stepchildren and step-grandchildren had fallen utterly under her spell and visited her submissively to be berated for their follies or approved for their good conduct, like the descendants of Louis XIV with his formidable morganatic spouse, Madame de Maintenon.

My hostess waited until Sylvia, who had greeted her with a quick kiss, had moved out of hearing, and then addressed me with a grave candor.

"It's not usual for Sylvia to ask to bring a man. You should be much complimented."

"Oh, but I am!"

"Well, I hope you're as nice as you look. Because I want somebody nice for Sylvia. She's had a hard time, that child. And she deserves a prince charming."

"Well, I can't claim to be a prince."

"But you'll provide the charm? Conceited fellow! Very well, we'll settle for that. But remember, if you don't treat her well, you'll have me to cope with!"

"Do I look such a creep, Mrs. Low?"

"No, you look like an angel. That's what worries me. And Sylvia tells me you've left your wife."

"As a matter of fact, she left me. And not even for another man. I guess she just couldn't stand me."

"Dear me, what did you do? But never mind. You can tell me at dinner. I've put you on my right." And leaving me thus dazzled, she turned to greet another guest.

As Sylvia moved from lady to lady — it was her custom, I discovered, to keep largely to her own sex in the cocktail hour — I had ample occasion to take in every detail of the great chamber. It was, as I now realize,

my first impression of perfect Louis XV, unless it should
have been called Pompadour, being free of the stateliness
and pomposity of so much of the royal decoration of
that century. The colors were a blend of sky blue, gold
apricot, pale peach, mauve pink, pomegranate, blue
green, and I don't know what else; the curtains and
panels and upholstery on which they were displayed
were shiningly clean. I noted that the high maintenance
of everything, paint, gilt and varnish, suggested that no
human had ever set a clumsy hand on them. And yet it
all still welcomed. Cupids smiled and flung garlands;
warblers seemed to twitter; angels beamed from fleecy
clouds. The central painting, by Boucher, over a "rose
Pompadour" divan, showed the famous mistress of the
king, with huge dark enigmatic eyes, gliding over blue
ice in a marvelously wrought sleigh drawn by two little
blackamoors on skates, her hands complacently folded
in an ermine muff. Sylvia told me later it was a replica
of the one at the Frick.

Mrs. Low, evidently, emulated the Pompadour. But
wasn't there a hint of the blue stocking in such perfect
taste? I thought I could see why the king had turned to
hot whores like Du Barry.

In the dining room, candles lit and gleaming, under
huge green and yellow tapestries of Alexander the
Great's victories in India, we seated ourselves at a long
table of twenty places laden with crystal wine glasses,
silver gilt plates and the porcelain centerpiece of a
Roman chariot race. Mrs. Low again gave me her grave
attention.

"You may be surprised, Mr. Service, that I take so personal an interest in your friendship with Sylvia. The dear girl has been very much on her own. Her courage and character in difficult times have been great indeed."

"I'm quite ready to take your word for that, Mrs. Low."

"My word? Aren't you ready to take your own?"

"Well, you see, I only met her this morning."

"This morning!" Mrs. Low's frank surprise was now converted into a throaty chuckle. "Well, well, it seems the cautious Sylvia can change her spots. You must have made a swift impression."

Seeing that it was no longer appropriate to speak to me as a possibly reluctant suitor who needed a push, my hostess now inquired about my life and antecedents, and in a few minutes possessed herself of an astonishing amount of information. Perhaps at one point in her long and eventful career she had been a personnel officer for a corporation. When the conversation changed, I turned to my other neighbor, a Hungarian cosmetics manufacturer, and listened as sympathetically as I knew how to the story of how she had cornered the market in a hair dye. I think our hostess must have been listening with her right ear, for before she rose when the meal was over she murmured to me:

"I think we're going to like you, Robert."

When the men joined the ladies in the parlor, I was glad to see that I was allowed to sit with Sylvia. Sipping my glass of champagne, I felt suddenly at ease and happy.

"Most of them work, don't they?" I asked, looking about at the guests. "Even the wives."

"What did you expect? Lascivious aristocrats, reclining on sofas? A Roman orgy?"

"Something like that. I hadn't realized to what extent New York society had become a working one. And I suppose they're all great successes at whatever it is they do?"

"Oh, yes. Ethelinda's nostrils are very sensitive to the stink of failure."

I nodded towards Mrs. Saunders, wife of the editor of *Town Voices*. "I suppose *she* doesn't work."

"She's not a failure, though. She caught Saunders."

"But isn't the real money hers?"

"That makes her even less of a failure. At Ethelinda's you don't have to have earned your success. You simply have to have it."

"What about me? Or is your success so great that your escort is admitted without question?"

"Oh, I'm not a success *here*. What are you thinking of? I'm simply supposed to be coming along. They always need recruits from the next generation. The toll of death and Florida is so high. And I think I've gone up a notch for bringing you. They like handsome young men who are clearly going to make it."

"Is it *that* clear?"

"Clear enough. You should have heard Ethelinda about you. And suppose you don't make it? What have they lost? Failure is quickly disposed of."

"It sounds like a hard world."

"Do you know a softer one?"

"No, I don't think I do. But suppose they take me in. Suppose I become a regular at this sort of gathering. What's in it for me?"

"Well, in the first place they're amusing. Probably more so than any other group in town. Because they have brains and do different things. You don't have one of those stultifying common denominators, like a profession or a suburb or even a cause. And secondly, you'll probably pick up a fair number of good clients."

"Do people really change lawyers because they meet someone they like at a dinner party?"

"You never can tell. Law and medicine have gotten so complicated that the best lawyers and doctors make terrible mistakes. These people hate mistakes. And the men, particularly, are inclined to grouse about it after a few drinks. Keep your ears open."

"As you do?"

"Oh, I'm always working. My office hours are my waking ones."

"That sounds like a terrible strain."

"You get used to it. For example, I'm perfectly happy and at ease right now. Yet I'm always aware of Mrs. Russo across the room. She's on the board of the Belvedere Hospital, and I know they're planning a drive."

"So you're ready to pounce?"

"I'm ready if she's ready. But I happen to know she doesn't like to talk business at a party. Still, it doesn't hurt to be awake."

"How did you get started in all this, Sylvia?"

"My father taught in a small backwater college in New Hampshire. He was able to get me a scholarship there, and I succeeded in marrying a boy from New York who couldn't get into Harvard, Yale or Princeton. People don't realize that the social advantages today are in the lesser-known schools. The Ivy League is full of poor geniuses who *may* become great. And who may not."

"I can't believe you're as worldly as you try to appear."

"I'm not. Or at least I wasn't. Tommy Sands came of an old and impoverished family that I found impossibly romantic. When we married, I had to go to work to support him."

"He did nothing?"

"He sold bonds when he could. He had no carry-through. Anyway, the poor darling died of leukemia when we had been married only five years."

"I'm sorry."

"So was I. But I should probably have been less so had it occurred later. He was beginning to drink."

"Ethelinda wouldn't have liked him."

"As a matter of fact, she did. None of us is wholly consistent. And then, he had charm."

"I'm surprised you haven't remarried."

"I have no rules about that. You'd better think twice before asking me."

"Oh, I shan't ask you."

She laughed. "How can you be so sure?"

"Because I'm still in love with Alice."

"Don't you know that's the surest way to make yourself attractive to a woman?"

"So help me, I'm naive!"

She looked at me almost as gravely as our hostess had. "I don't know if you are or aren't. You're a funny one, my friend."

When I took her home I asked if I could come up for a nightcap. She hesitated.

"You'll have to be very quiet and not wake up Tommy."

"Oh, I can be like a cat."

"Maybe that's what I'm afraid of."

Upstairs in her small beautiful apartment, crowded with every kind of bibelot, with red-lacquered Chinese furniture and scroll paintings, she told me to mix myself a drink while she checked on her son. When she returned she was clad in a white silk nightgown and a blue kimono.

"You're a remarkable man, Mr. Service. You've made me break every rule I've made for myself in the past six years. I asked you out to dinner the same day we met, and now I'm going to let you spend the night. Or a part of the night. If you care to, that is. I'm following a hunch. Who knows? It may turn out to be the idea lousy. And then again it may not."

It definitely did not turn out to be the idea lousy. Sylvia as a lover managed to be both hot and cool, moving her slim body with astounding grace. At our moment of climax, however, she let out a cry that was soon followed by a knock at the door.

"Are you all right, Mummy?" a boy's voice called.

"Yes, darling, only a nightmare," she responded with perfect equanimity. "Go back to bed, dear."

But immediately afterwards she made me dress in the dark and depart on tip-toe.

"Did you pretend I was your wife?" she whispered.

"No!"

"Thank you." And she gave me a quick parting kiss. I knew that a novel and extraordinary thing had entered my life.

· 12 ·

THE NOVEL THING certainly changed my humdrum existence in the next three months. As I look back over them it seems that I had little time to think, only to be. I certainly had no opportunity to make notes in this journal. At the office I was as busy as ever, and many of my evenings and weekends were still devoted to law work, but the balance of the former were now dedicated to accompanying Sylvia on her nocturnal rounds. We went to dinner parties, to openings, to charity balls. In the interims we managed to make love, not in my room at the Stafford, which I had given up when Sylvia dubbed it "tacky," or in her apartment, where her son was not again to be disturbed, but in the small, furnished floor of a brownstone that I had found and sublet. I thought it adequately attractive, but Sylvia was never content with it, and every time she arrived it was with a print or a jar or a bed cover, something, anything, to tone up its "dullness."

I don't know why she bothered. She never came to
the little place except to do one thing, and that, as often
as not, was done in the dark. Sylvia became a different
person when she made love. She never spoke or uttered
a sound unless it was such a cry of satisfaction as had
awakened her son; she might have been going through
some sort of gymnastic exercise, necessary for her well-
being but not to be acknowledged or even spoken of.
Was it love? Anyway, I felt that she cared very much
about pleasing me. And I always knew at parties that,
even though she never seemed to be looking at me, she
was aware of everything I did. It was clear that I had
come to play an important role in her life, but she
wouldn't discuss it — just as she wouldn't discuss anything abstract: religion, an afterlife, the deeper meaning
of things. Sylvia lived for the here and now as did no
epicurean I had ever known, and she was quite as serious
about it as my hero, Marius. With her the moment not
only had to be lived for; it had to be created. As she
used to say, if a poor widow with a child to support
didn't look after herself, who would?

Well, wouldn't I? Wasn't that what she had to be
thinking? Wasn't I being groomed to be the consort of
Sylvia Sands? What kept me from worrying too much
about it was the peculiar confidence that she inspired in
me that, whatever she wanted and however near she
might come to obtaining it, she would never insist. She
might say in the end: "Well, here it is. Do you want it
or don't you?" and if the answer was in the negative,
she might simply shrug, perhaps with a bit of a frown,

and turn to other fields. This quality in her struck me as gratifyingly unfeminine, for I still believed that women were more designing in the sexual game than men. I found that I trusted Sylvia as I should have trusted one of my own sex.

The society into which she introduced me is difficult to define, except that it was obviously the highest in town. There are many New York societies. There are the descendants of old families who huddle over backgammon and bridge tables in the Union, Knickerbocker and Colony clubs; there are the worlds of the cultural institutions and of academe; there are tycoons of unfathomed new wealth, who tend to dwell in semi-isolation, surrounded by little "courts." Sylvia's society included some of the very rich, but not necessarily the richest, with a few old names and a lot of new, and it seemed loosely united by the determination, at least in its women, to look beautiful, even in advanced age, and to live beautifully, with the best in art and decoration. But its members also contributed substantially to the cultural and charitable institutions of the city, and they managed the businesses that affected public thought: broadcasting, newspapers, theatres, publishing firms. They were much written up in the media, and they tended to speak of one another in hyperbolic terms: "Isn't Ethelinda wonderful?" or "Don't you just adore Lila?" I wondered if ever before had an upper class been so civic-minded. Even if they were so only because it had become the thing to be, they were still beneficent.

Sylvia, as I soon perceived, had only one real entrée

into this world, and that was Mrs. Low, but that was quite enough. She had been almost adopted by the old lady; they talked on the telephone every morning, and people had learned that at large parties the great Ethelinda liked to be assured of a small circle of intimates of whom Sylvia was definitely one. And "great" Ethelinda was rightly called. It was not only the way she gave away chunks of the fortune that Low had left her outright and that, childless, she had no reason to hoard; it was the almost formidable exquisiteness of the great gilded shells that she had constructed for herself in New York, Southampton and Palm Beach, and in the happy hand she showed in filling them with amusing and active people. Ethelinda was without illusions and without pretensions; she had a sharp eye, a rough tongue and a kind heart. There were friends of her late husband, I heard, who sneered at her origins and expressed amazement at the people who flocked to her door, but Ethelinda's group gave only moderate marks to background and lineage. Such assets were never tickets of entry by themselves.

She was certainly very candid about her plans for Sylvia.

"I am going to set up a charitable trust on my death," she told me one night at dinner. "I promised my husband that I would do so, and of course I shall be good to my word. He had already looked after his children and grandchildren, so I needn't be concerned with them. I shall feel free to leave legacies to my friends, but mostly of works of art. I am leaving Sylvia the little Boudin

beach scene that she admires, but more importantly I plan
to make her a trustee of my trust. It will be she who will
be doing me the favor. That girl will have an x-ray eye
to spot the phonies among the applicants."

Sylvia was pleased, later that night, to hear that Mrs.
Low had confided to me her plans for her will. She was
quite aware of them herself. She was also aware, I discovered, of the difference between a foundation, whose
directors might receive only a nominal compensation,
and Ethelinda's proposed charitable trust, whose fiduci-
aries would earn substantial commissions.

"You're really getting on with her wonderfully," she
said approvingly. "But we have to remember that although she talks about changing her will, she hasn't
done so yet. Gil Arnheim, her lawyer, keeps putting it
off."

"He's probably put himself in the old one as a trustee
and doesn't want to share with you."

"Well, he might not so much mind sharing. What
he's afraid of is being replaced."

I did not altogether like the faint menace in Sylvia's
tone. Now why was that? Was I being a male chauvinist?
Why should she not be just as calculating as I? She
should, of course. I changed to a lighter subject.

"Do you think Ethelinda's taking the trouble to
correct my language is a sign of favor?" I asked.

"How did she do that?"

"When I said I was taking you to my parents' 'home'
for the weekend, she said, 'You mean, their house.' And
she wrinkled her nose when I referred to the new cur-

tains in her living room as 'drapes.' Is there a special vocabulary for society?"

"I suppose that dates Ethelinda. I wouldn't worry about it. When she had to break her way in forty years ago, the old Knickerbocker families could still be pretty silly about terminology. But even then, if they liked you, you could call an evening dress a 'formal' and get away with it."

"Why shouldn't I call an evening dress a 'formal'?"

"Go ahead, if you want. A handsome young man who's getting on can say almost anything."

"What about a handsome young woman?"

"Oh, women always have to do better."

"That doesn't seem very fair."

"I don't bother with what's fair and unfair. All I need to know is the rules."

"So you think I can just relax and be myself?"

"I'd put it even more strongly. I think you *must* relax and be yourself. It's the only way to crack the world you're trying to crack."

"So there *is* a world I'm trying to crack?"

"Of course there is, silly. You're not 'in' with a handful of dinner parties. Any extra man can be asked to dinner."

"You're not forgetting that I'm a working man, are you?"

"My beautiful boy, isn't it precisely the thing that I *am* remembering? In the great world, you must learn, there's no difference between work and play."

I had few moments those days to think of myself and

where I was going. If I worked three nights a week, I
was in a black tie others, and when I took Sylvia home
after a stop-off at my flat I was so tired as to sleep a
dreamless sleep. Yet there was a kind of narcotic in my
busy-ness. I liked my work; I liked meeting important
people in gilded dining rooms; I liked making love to
Sylvia. Was I falling in love? I do not think in that period
I often asked myself the question. Perhaps a man is not
so apt to ask it if the woman doesn't.

The office was much amused when a photograph of
me dancing with Sylvia appeared in *Women's Wear
Daily*. But if my reputation soared with the stenographic
staff it did not do so with the sardonic Douglas Hyde,
who spent such evenings as he could spare from his law
labors with his wife and six young children in their house
in Scarsdale.

"I see we're moving in the highest society," he observed caustically.

"We can't all stay in Dullsville. Some of us have to
get around."

"And I note there's a big do at the St. Regis Roof
tonight. No doubt you'll be there."

"As a matter of fact, I shall."

"Why not? I can take over the closing dinner for Ace
Investors."

I saw that Douglas was not being wholly humorous.
He believed that I should be at that dinner. In a sudden
fit of compunction, and feeling, too, that Sylvia and her
friends were beginning to take me a bit for granted, I
decided to change my plans. I called Sylvia's office and

told her secretary that I had to give out of the St. Regis party. It was ominous that she did not call back.

When I rang her the next morning she refused to pick up the telephone, and her secretary gently chided me.

"I'm afraid we're mad at you, Mr. Service. Where were you last night?"

"I had an emergency at the office."

There was a pause while she consulted Sylvia.

"Mrs. Sands says you *may* be forgiven if you meet her for lunch at twelve-thirty at the Amboise."

"But she knows we have a firm lunch today . . . Wait! Okay. Tell her I'll be there."

At lunch Sylvia was benign but firm.

"There's one thing, my dear, you must get straight. This evening life I'm arranging for you is a serious thing. I grant that the people whose parties we go to would not hesitate to throw you over if business or even pleasure interfered. But they do not expect to be thrown over themselves. For any reason. That's the difference. The day will come when you can do as they do, but that day is not yet. And in the meanwhile you must stop telling people how hard you work. They don't care. Besides, it's the mark of an underling. A big man is master of his time."

"Sylvia, darling, I appreciate what you're doing for me, believe me. But sometimes I think you don't understand that what really builds up a law practice is expertise and hard work."

"Of course I know that. Do you take me for a complete ass? But just look in *Martindale's* at the number of lawyers swarming up and down this skinny island. Do you think I can't find a dozen experts ready and willing to take on any job that Robert Service can handle?"

"I'm afraid you can."

"Very well, then, face it. Getting the business is half the job. Unless you're such a wizard the whole world flocks to your door. You'd be surprised if you knew how many queries I've already had about you."

"Really? And what do you say?"

"That you're the best — but very expensive."

"With all due respect, I haven't noticed that any have come calling."

"Give them time, honey. You remember Alva, the cosmetician? She's thinking of coming to you for a will. And she'll probably put you in it if you'll only slide your hand up her leg under the table — well above the knee!"

"That old fortress! You wouldn't have me do that, would you, Sylvia? Seriously?"

"No." She laughed at my worried eyes. "But it's important for you to know the effect you have on people. Otherwise you can't use it. Admit I've been reasonable, Bob. I haven't overworked you, have I? You have plenty of nights for the law. Probably too many. And look at you. Fresh as a daisy!"

As I looked at her, so smoothly smiling, so relaxed, perhaps so happy — how did I know? — and yet still so aware of where she was and who else might be at what table, so eager to look after my wants, my needs, my soul — why not? — I felt I was a churl not to meet her terms.

"I'll be good," I promised. "Only let's order. I have to be back in the office."

"Leave it to me," she said, catching the eye of the headwaiter. "You'll be out of here in exactly thirty-five minutes."

· 13 ·

IN THE SHORT TIME that these things take in our culture, Sylvia's and my lives began to blend into domesticity. On weekends we would take our children to walk in Central Park. I was not at all sure that Audrey and Sally liked Sylvia, but they were certainly intrigued by her. She seemed to make no effort to gain their affection; she treated them with the same calm, mildly amiable objectivity that was her manner with adults. But I thought I could glean the secret of her success in that she never asked them a perfunctory question. When she sought an answer to something she gave every appearance not only of wanting it but of insisting on getting it. Children do not like to feel their time is being wasted. My daughters respected Sylvia; they may even have been afraid of her. She showed none of the vulnerability of needing to be loved by children that children can smell as sharks smell blood. I was actually proud of her, noting that when we walked in the park, Audrey and Sally held themselves as straight as she did.

Sylvia's son, Tommy Sands, was a beautiful, delicate and enchanting child of ten, very blond and pale, who seemed to have no Hamlet complex. On the contrary, he was inclined to take my hand on our strolls instead of his mother's. Obviously the poor child was dying to have a daddy like his friends, and he saw no reason that I should not do. I was charmed, of course. In some ways I felt closer to the gravely confiding Tommy than to his sometimes impenetrable mother.

One Saturday afternoon when I took the girls back to Alice's apartment, she sent them to their room and invited me to have a drink. Alice was wearing an unfamiliar air; she seemed determined to be bright, cheerful and, well, I guess polite.

"There's something I don't quite know how to say, Bob."

"About some man you're seeing?" I was startled at the instant grating of jealousy in my tone.

"Why no, not at all," she retorted, surprised. "It's quite the opposite, as a matter of fact. Of course, I've heard that you were going about with Mrs. Sands. Naturally, the girls have told me, and —"

"I hope they were polite about her."

"Very polite, Bob. Don't be so on the defensive. Nobody's objecting to your seeing Mrs. Sands. After all, when I walked out, I could hardly expect you to live like a monk. No, what I'm trying to tell you is that if you and Mrs. Sands find me an obstacle, I'm perfectly willing to get out of your way."

I looked darkly at those candid eyes. For a minute I

did not know what to do with the anger that I felt jumping about inside me. It was as if I had risen to make a public address and found that somebody was trying to pull my pants off. At last I arose and walked to the window. When I felt in control of myself again I asked, "You're trying to tell me you'll give me a divorce?"

"If you want one."

"And if I don't want one?"

"You mean if I'm a convenience and not an obstacle? Perhaps even a protection to you? Poor Mrs. Sands! And I thought she seemed so nice."

"You know her?"

"She came to see me. Didn't she tell you? She thought we should have a talk because of Audrey and Sally. I considered that very sympathetic of her."

"Well, I'll be damned! Is that how a man's disposed of behind his back?"

"Don't be absurd. She simply wanted to know if I had any pointers on how to handle the girls. If there were any particular topics to avoid, or good ones to bring up. She's obviously a very intelligent woman."

"Maybe you're the one who wants the divorce," I went on wrathfully, ignoring what she had said. "Maybe you've found a man you want to marry. I don't suppose it's one of your poets, anyway. Their tastes are not for your sex, are they? Or would they put up with a woman to share in the settlement they hope you'll get out of me?"

Alice looked away, embarrassed by my crudeness. "I

guess you'd better go, Bob. I was only trying to be helpful."

I looked miserably around the little room where I had once been so happy. Or at least where I had thought myself happy. The chintz on the sofa looked faded, and the clock on the mantel had stopped. Alice was poor! She was poor and wouldn't take anything from me. The stained old lithograph of the Empress Elizabeth of Austria by Winterhalter was evidence of her absence of taste, her total indifference to decoration. Sylvia wouldn't have lived with it, even for a night. But it broke my heart.

"I wish I was dead," I muttered.

"Bob, Bob, don't talk like that!"

"I still love you! In spite of everything."

"Please! You have a fixation about me. It's because you can't bear to fail in anything. You've got to develop some objectivity."

"If you send me back to Sylvia now, it may be forever."

"I'm not sending you back to Sylvia. I'm not sending you back to anyone. I want to find out what you are and what I am."

"You want to find out why the hell you married me! That's the long and short of it, isn't it?"

Alice folded her arms across her breast with a sigh. "All right, let it go at that. I want to find out why the hell I married you."

When I taxed Sylvia that night with her visit to Alice, she took a high stand.

"That's the kind of thing women do, my dear, and

you had better learn to leave it to us. One way or another we have to put your house in order."

When I took Sylvia out to Keswick for a Sunday lunch with Mother and Dad, they behaved politely, but the occasion was still a chilly one. It was certainly not Sylvia's fault. She showed an irreproachable interest in my parents' lives and what they did, and never betrayed by a single reference the fact that she moved in more exalted social spheres. It was manifest to me that my progenitors disapproved of her, and it finally made me indignant. How could they be so absurd as to view her, a hard-working widow who supported her child, as a kind of whore of Babylon? Nor did I make things any better by touting, despite Sylvia's veiled pucker of a frown, her professional accomplishments.

"In my opinion, Dad, Sylvia's most remarkable work has been with institutions that had developed a pinkish look in the McCarthy era. She gives them a new look by getting their officers to build up a record of anti-communist statements made at periodic intervals over a span of time. When she's through with them they might look to a grant from the John Birch Society!"

Dad was determined to be pleasant, but there was nonetheless a jibe in his response. "I guess she's like the duchess in *The Gondoliers* who cleans up the lady of doubtful propriety. Is that it, Mrs. Sands?" And he proceeded to intone:

> "Where virtue would quash her,
> I take and whitewash her,
> And launch her in first-rate society!"

"I wonder if it's ever really worthwhile," Mother observed bleakly, "to cajole or fool people into giving away their money."

"Most of the cultural institutions of this country would turn their faces to the wall under that theory!" I retorted.

"Maybe Mrs. Service thinks that would be a good thing," Sylvia observed in a tone that implied that she might agree with Mother.

I suppose there was an irony in my seeking to persuade Mother that Sylvia was a "nice" woman. As a boy I had violently resisted her and Father's constant inclusion of their friends and neighbors under the porous umbrella of that loose and sentimental term. I remember how cynically I used to react to the rushing together of their windy feelings in their obvious desire to inculcate a cynical son with some iota of virtue, as when one would say to the other across the dining room table, with a meaningful glance in my direction, "Well, I don't care what people say. I think the Ameses are *nice* people," or, "Isn't Mr. Cox the *nicest* man you've ever known?" or perhaps more simply and explosively and even more absurdly, "Aren't people *nice!*" And I would huddle lower in my chair, a retracting turtle, and blink from one to the other of them balefully, defiantly, until Mother would say to Dad in a tone of deep concern: "I'm afraid what Bob needs is a simple lesson in Christian principles!"

It was never, of course, that I thought *they* were not nice or even that they were not sincere in deeming others possessed of this nebulous quality. What made me gnash my teeth was the way they insisted on seeing their oppressors as benevolent guardians: the partners of Dad's firm who had extracted the last ounce of work out of him for a miserable stipend, my demanding maternal grandmother, who had lived with us until her dying day, making Dad feel a guest in his own home, and some of the richer Westchester neighbors who used Mother like a slave on their charity drives and never once asked the Services to break bread in their mansions.

And yet here I was, twisting my cap, so to speak, into a rag between my knees, like some tense sixteen-year-old bringing his first date to Ma and Pa in the hope of some dim expression of approval! I should have been enchanted to settle for a single "nice." But did I get one?

"Mrs. Sands, I'm sure, is a brilliant woman," was Mother's ultimate concession, imparted to me after lunch while Dad was showing Sylvia his tiny rose garden.

Of course, she filled me with angry doubts. What mother cannot do that? Who *was* Sylvia, as the bard asked? Did she even exist? I had read the Canadian, McLuhan, who, so far as I could make out, maintained that truth was only what most people believed at a particular time. Thus, Alger Hiss could be guilty or innocent at different periods. Perhaps what McLuhan meant was that people's ideas of what constituted a crime varied at different times, so that what wasn't a crime in the 1940s became one under Joe McCarthy. Or did he actually mean that a particular act, say, the copying of an official document, happened or failed to happen depending on what people thought?

Sylvia, like one playing an instrument in an orchestra,

seemed to be taking her cue from a conductor. But who was he? She seemed to have no opinions herself on how the piece should be played, or even to consider that some conductors might be better than others. Yet she never appeared weak or faltering; her very refusal to be involved gave her a certain force of character. In her heart she seemed to stand aside, even when her mind was most active. But do not hearts atrophy if they are left indefinitely in the wings?

And who was I to blame her? Was I not committing adultery, at least twice a week, as casually as playing squash at the University Club? Would I not be more interesting, at least to myself, if I underwent some throes of guilt? When I turned to an author whom I admire almost as much as I do Pater — Hawthorne — I could see that the incomparable beauty of *The Scarlet Letter* lies in Hester's brooding sense of guilt, which permeates her vision of the town, the forest and the grim faces of her persecutors. Guilt over what? At having made love to a beautiful minister of God at a time when she was poor and abandoned, and believed her husband dead? No. Hester accepted the harsh judgment of her peers not so much as a judgment as a fact. It was hers; it was *she*; she had to live with it, for it had made her. And I was living without guilt, like Sylvia. Was that what made us both at times seem a bit dry?

· 14 ·

I found that I was becoming as close to Ethelinda as Sylvia, if not closer. The old lady wanted us both to be with her as much as possible, and she asked us for weekends at the great white glistening villa on the dunes in Southampton, transporting us painlessly thither in her little jet, but she also wanted me to lunch with her alone, and she took to telephoning me at the office to relay bits of gossip she had just heard or funny stories that were often quite unclean. Sylvia showed not the slightest jealousy; on the contrary she encouraged our intimacy. She put me in mind of Kate Croy, in James's *Wings of the Dove*, nurturing Merton Densher's romantic friendship with the dying heiress, Milly Theale, in order that he might inherit her fortune and share it with Kate. But surely Sylvia was not planning to marry me to Mrs. Low! Ethelinda was splendidly preserved, but, judging from the few biographical facts I had gleaned, she had to be eighty.

I was getting to know her pretty well. She had great qualities, but she had weaknesses, too. If she ran her establishments as tautly as naval vessels, with ashtrays emptied almost as the first cinder fell, with cushions plumped up the moment a sitter rose, if she remembered the favorite dish and conversational topic of every guest of honor, if she studied her city politics and contributed to every honest candidate, if she toured slums and hospitals to check the effects of her bounty, she had also an avid ear for scandal and a near terror of loneliness. She would do anything to avoid a solitary evening. Although she was supposed to be a difficult target for a social climber, she made herself shamelessly available to anyone who offered to fill a stubborn vacancy in her calendar. "Oh, we mustn't be stuffy; we must meet the new people," she would retort if Sylvia protested that she was dining with thugs. And I also began to note that Ethelinda's concern with maintenance was verging on the obsessive. She would redecorate new and shining chambers on the ground that they were "shabby." It was as if she wanted to scrub and clean the gilded shells with which she covered her old bones until she could crawl into heaven itself.

"Think what her childhood must have been like," was Sylvia's comment when I mentioned this. "She can never have enough beauty around her to shut out the memory of all that dirt and squalor."

"Does she ever talk about it?"

"Never. Not that she conceals it. She will say, 'You can't imagine, darling, what a sty I came from.' But then she shuts it out, muttering, 'One of the reasons I can do things for the poor and wretched is that I know how little can be done.' "

I also began to observe that the old girl's memory was going. One day when she and I were lunching alone at the Amboise, she betrayed a notable lapse.

"People have no idea what a job it is to give away money. They think you ought to be able to spot flatterers by their oiliness. They don't realize that the worst liars are the presidents of our great universities and museums. Because these men think it's morally justifiable to do anything under the sun for a good cause. Look at David King sitting over there, smiling smugly at that man — what's his name? — from the Colonial Museum. Can't you just see David's swallowing every word he's being told? And he's so puffed up, too, about running his own foundation. 'Why do I need a great staff, like Ford?' he asks. 'Does it take any more time to write a check for a hundred g's than one for a million?' Very amusing. And all New York worships David. So generous! So great-hearted! But I'll bet he gets taken to the cleaners on half his grants."

"He should be like the Ford Foundation, then, and have more staff?"

"Well, Ford's the opposite extreme. Too many people, too many reports. And that quaint dread of public opinion that foundations should be exempt from and aren't at all. No, I tell you, Bob, when I die, I'm going to leave what I have to half a dozen institutions that I believe in, to do with as they choose. Let them cut the lawn or build buildings, what does it matter? They're going to find a way to get around your restrictions, anyway. All you can do is pick the best, and, mind you, the best won't be any too good."

"But, Ethelinda," I protested, "what became of your idea of the charitable trust? With Sylvia as a trustee?"

"Charitable trust? Sylvia? What are you talking about, dear boy? You're thinking of some other old gal you were making up to after too many cocktails. I'm going to tell Sylvia she's taking you out too much."

I did not press the point and allowed her to tell me about David King's handsome young male secretary who was leading his boss by the nose . . .

"Nose, did you say?"

"Oh, Robert, you're terrible!"

I told Sylvia that night that I had found our great lady a bit tired.

"Tired? Did she say anything in particular?"

"She didn't seem to remember anything about our charitable trust discussion. Not a word."

"Of course, she's old. And older than people think."

"Yes, but is she. . . ?"

"What?"

"Well, entirely all there?"

"Look here, Bob." Sylvia turned on me now, very firm. "Ethelinda's mind is as good as yours or mine. Her memory may be slipping a bit. But that doesn't mean she's non compos."

"Until it slips altogether. It's one thing if you forget what you had for dinner last night. It's another when you forget the question before you can answer it."

"Ethelinda's a long way from that."

"All right, all right! Why be so grim about it?"

"Because she's talking about naming you as well as me a trustee of her trust."

"Are you serious?"

"And Gil Arnheim. The three of us. I know she's been discussing it with him."

"But you told me he was dragging his feet. Maybe he's worried about her testamentary capacity."

"No, it's not that at all. It's because he doesn't want to see us cut in on his business. The people who control Ethelinda's trust are going to be persons to reckon with in this town. And we'll be two out of three!"

"Meaning that we would use the power of philanthropy to advance ourselves in the world?"

"No, dear, no." Sylvia sighed as if she were dealing with a tedious child. "How many times have you told me that you're honest to a fault? You shouldn't rub it in so. It might make people wonder. And I ought to resent your insinuation that I'm in any way less scrupulous than you. Let me simply assure you that the trust will be scrupulously run. We'll be the ones who are running it, that's all. Ethelinda, in the full possession of her faculties, will change her will to name you and Arnheim as executors and you and me and Arnheim as trustees. And it's very important that we all believe her to be of sound mind!"

"Even if she isn't?"

"Bob, I think I'll kill you if you destroy my scheme! It's so beautiful. Ethelinda will be of fully sound mind when she executes that will. Believe me! Neither Arn-

heim nor I will allow her to do it on one of her bad days.
You know, as a lawyer, that a person can have sane and
less sane moments. Isn't that so?"

"I suppose so."

"Then it's a question of picking the right one, isn't
it?"

"Unless the testator shouldn't execute a will at all.
What about the family? Won't they contest?"

"You mean Ethelinda's own nieces and nephews? She
has some, actually. No. Because they're getting substantial cash legacies that will lapse if they contest. And
if they should contest and by a miracle knock out the
will, they'd only revive an older one that also leaves
everything to charity. So they'll shut up and take their
bequests."

"I see. It fits. But why does Mr. Arnheim go along
with you?"

"Because he's still going to be an executor and trustee."

"And he's afraid of what you might do if he doesn't
cooperate?"

"Of course he is. Even though I wouldn't do a thing.
But I don't have to tell him that, do I? Can't I leave him
to his own ruminations? You see, I *know* that Ethelinda,
most of the time, wants this alteration in her will. She
may change her mind, but is that any reason that her
present, perfectly rational plan shouldn't be imple-
mented? Particularly when not a penny less will go to
charity? The only change will be that you and I become persons of consequence. Is that a crime?"

Well, was it? The admirable creature had thought it

all out. Her scheme was foolproof. The Lows were not Ethelinda's heirs-at-law or next of kin; they had no right to contest. And her own relatives were quieted with legacies and the prospect of losing all if they so much as peeped. Who lost? Nobody. The charitable trust would come into being under the new will. Only Sylvia Sands and Robert Service would mark the difference, and was anyone the worse if they had a hand in honestly and conscientiously distributing the treasure? Of course not. And the eyes of all New York would be on Sylvia and Robert.

"It fits," I repeated. "It fits almost too well. But won't we get commissions?"

"And why not? Shall we not earn them? For don't misunderstand me, Bob. I expect to be a very good trustee!"

Could anyone doubt it? Not I.

· 15 ·

In the meantime I was having my troubles in the office. It was probably because, strapped between my law work and social life, I had less time for firm management. I had even been known to miss a partners' lunch, leaving the sardonic Doug Hyde to act as chairman in my place. But even when I had missed a meeting, I felt entitled to review any actions taken by those attending. After all, according to my calculations, I was now directly responsible for sixty-five per cent of the billings of the firm.

Doug warned me that there was trouble afoot. Some of the younger partners were beginning to resent what they termed my "arbitrariness." Their leader was a thirty-year-old, the newest partner, brought forward, alas, by myself, one Oswald Burley, a tall, bony, good-looking "whiz kid," a *Harvard Law Review* man, the son of a federal judge, who had joined us instead of one of the greater firms because he deemed us more "up and coming" and who had taken it upon himself, from the first day of his membership in the firm, to address us as if he had been a founding father.

He did not hesitate to challenge the direction in which I was leading the partners, dubbing it the "march to uniformity." He warned not only the partners but the associates that lawyers everywhere were losing their sense of the profession as a noble and learned calling and allowing it to degenerate into "just another business." What particularly irritated me was that "Oz," as he was called, appeared to have no recognition of how galling his homilies were to me. He took it for granted that we were all what he termed "men of good will" and that it could only take a few candid and open conversations before even Bob Service would come over to his side. He had a lot to learn.

"It won't do to underrate Oz," Doug warned me. "He seems to cast a kind of spell over the younger partners."

I knew that Doug was the strongest support I had in the office. He was slower and more easygoing than I, so he inspired a greater trust, but behind that impassive, sober countenance and the occasional mocking glint in his eye lay a firm conviction that I was running a taut ship and one on which he could depend to bring a greater prosperity to Douglas Hyde, the ambitious father of six little boys.

"I wish he'd use his curious spell to bring in new clients," I retorted.

"You know what might be a smart move? To put him on the executive committee."

"Have you lost your marbles?"

"No. I'm quite serious. If you put him on the committee all the lower-point partners will feel they have a voice there. And you'll still have an easy majority. Think it over."

"I tell you right now. The day he goes on that committee, I go off!"

Doug shook his head. "That's not the way to handle him. You've got to learn to compromise, Bob."

"Compromise? From a position of power?"

"Yes. While you still have it."

"Doug, you don't seem to realize that this firm needs me a hell of a lot more than I need it."

"Okay. But people do strange things if they think they're being kicked around."

"They're not being kicked around."

"I said, if they think they are."

Certainly Oz Burley showed no signs of "going away." He took to haranguing us at firm lunches as if we were a seminar gathered to heed the words of a wise professor. Even his good temper aroused my ire. He was so reasonable, and he expected us to be equally reasonable. His pale thin handsome face, bent over the notes that he had the boldness to bring to the table, his hesitations that somehow kept pace with his stubborn reiterations, his air of bland assumption that we lived, didn't we, in an enlightened sector of a dark universe, maddened me. How did he have the nerve to put himself, created by me, in *my* category? But he did. Here is a sample of his ranting:

"I think I should bring to the firm's attention that

some of the biggest law partnerships in the country are opting for an even distribution of profits. When you're elected a partner under such a system, it takes you a while, say three or four years, to work up to the norm, and when you're old and about to retire, you work down, or 'phase out' over an equal period, but for most of your productive life you share evenly with your partners. It's to me a very attractive idea. We should all be working for the same goal. The fact that one of us happens to have lost a difficult case while another has had a large estate fall in shouldn't vary our remuneration. One should assume that all partners are doing their best."

What was it about him that brought out the worst in me? I heard myself calling down the table, "What's the difference between your system, Oz, and the one devised by Lenin for the Soviet Union?"

"Simply this. That our 'communism,' if that be the right term, is a private agreement and not one imposed by the state. If each partner in a lucrative firm were to receive half a million in income, he could hardly call himself a proletariat."

"But the partner who goofs off gets as much as the one who sweats his ass to bring in the clients!"

"The partner who goofs off should soon cease to be a partner," Oz retorted coolly. "I am assuming a firm in which we all pull together. If a client doesn't pay, we should give the client up, unless there's some *pro bono* or public relations reason for holding on to him. And if that's the case, why should the partner stuck with that client be penalized? Consider it, gentlemen.

Wouldn't it be pleasant to practice law without having to think every minute if you're charging as many hours as Bob Service?"

The murmur around the table established that he had made a point.

It was not long after this that, as foreseen by Doug, a serious movement got under way to put Oz Burley on the executive committee. I let it be known that I should resign from the committee if this occurred, but this did not have the deterrent effect that I had anticipated.

"Face it, Bob," Doug warned me. "The younger men don't really care if you get off the committee. They think you're getting too bossy. Of course, if they thought you'd quit the firm, they'd give up about Oz. But they figure you're not going to do that. They figure it wouldn't be worth your while to break up the firm on so small an issue."

"Maybe they don't know me," I said grimly.

"Well, it wouldn't be worth it, would it? And, as a matter of fact, it might be easier to control Oz on the committee than off."

"That's not the point, Doug. The point is that I've worked my tail off to create a firm that operates efficiently. And I didn't do it to have to justify myself to a young snotnose every time I sneeze or take a leak."

"Well, if it comes to a vote, I think you may lose."

"Do you mean it?"

"Narrowly but possibly."

Sylvia and I were dining that night at Ethelinda's, and for once I dreaded the party. But she told me that

Ethelinda, too, was tired and wanted me to sit with her after dinner in a corner of the library. There was only room for one on the small sofa beside her, and when I was seated there she indulged in the unusual gesture of stroking my hand. I gazed into her eyes and then down at those long brown speckled fingers. Smiling, she released me.

"Forgive me, dear. I am just warming my old bones at the fire of your young life. You and Sylvia have it all before you. Ah, well, I can't complain. I've had most of it myself. The great thing is not to have wasted your life. So many do."

"You mean you've done everything you wanted?" Her air of somber reflection made me suddenly as serious as she. "Everything you've really wanted to do?"

"I think so. Though for a time I had to do things I didn't want, to get to where I had a choice."

"What sort of things?"

"Isn't that a rather personal question, young man?"

"I suppose it's very personal. But you're a great woman, Ethelinda, which means that everything that went into you has to be worth knowing. Why should I waste our precious time in chitchat?"

This gratified her. "You have a point. Let me tell you this, then. You may have noticed that I am a great admirer of this lady." She reached a hand to touch the porcelain bust of Madame de Pompadour in a niche between the red morocco volumes on the shelf behind her. "I guess I've read all there is to read about her. And do you know the most interesting fact in her story? She was cold."

"You mean cold-hearted?"

"No, dear boy. Cold as a lover. Cold in bed. She had to put it on, even with the king, who was a veteran lover and hard to fool. How relieved she must have been when she discovered that she could keep his heart and give his body to the little harlots of the Parc aux Cerfs. Now all of France was hers to play with: gardens and palaces and paintings and statues and books and plays and music. And how much she made of it all!"

But I held her to the point. "Did you have a deer park for Mr. Low?"

"Come, Robert, are there no limits?"

"Should there be? Among friends? Real friends?"

She weighed this. Then she shrugged. "Anyway, Sidney was too old when I married him to need anything like that. But my second husband . . . well, *je ne dis pas!*"

"And your first?"

"Ah, that was love."

"And all the time, even in the early days, you knew, you were sure, that if you could ever get everything you wanted, it would be wonderful?"

"Yes, I did. And it was."

"That *is* wonderful."

"You don't think it would be so with you?"

I hesitated. But she had been frank. I owed it to her. "No."

"Your life is like those advertisements for the ocean liners: 'Getting there is half the fun'?"

"Getting there is all the fun."

"Dear me. Well, then, let's hope you never get there. That your life will be one long cruise."

I made the mistake of persisting. I really wanted to know. After all, what *was* I working for? Ethelinda seemed to have turned into a python, an oracle. She was Delphi itself. "You're sure that you love all your beautiful things for themselves? For their own intrinsic beauty?" I asked.

"What else?"

"You're sure it's in no way for what they do for you? I mean for the splendid background they make for Ethelinda Low? Oh, I know that sounds bad, but I can't help wondering if any of us can ever really get out of ourselves. And if anyone could tell me, it would be you!"

"I don't know what you're talking about, and I'm not at all sure that I want to."

I quickly changed the subject to gossip and kept it there for the rest of the evening. I hoped that I had obliterated the bad impression, but I hadn't. In the taxi Sylvia demanded, "What in God's name were you doing to Ethelinda? When I said good night, she complained you'd accused her of buying pictures to show people how rich she was."

"I didn't quite say that." I tried to explain what I had said, but it didn't come out very differently.

"I take it Ethelinda hit the nail on the head."

"Well, can't we ever be serious in this world of yours?" I complained, exasperated. "Don't you ever get starved for a bit of truth?"

"Like Benchley's remedy for the urge to take exercise, I lie down till the feeling goes away. How many times do I have to tell you that you can't indulge your personal feelings till you get to the top of the heap?"

"Maybe I won't want to then."

"Maybe not. That's the chance you take."

"I'm sorry, Sylvia. I guess I was too tired to go out tonight. I had a bad day at the office."

"Mr. Burley again?"

"How did you guess?"

"Because I'm getting to know you, dear, like a book." We had reached her house. "Come up for a drink and tell me about it. Just one drink and just that. We're both tired."

She listened to me in her still, attentive way as I related the iniquities of Oz Burley. I knew that she didn't in the least comprehend why it was so important to me to run my firm as I wanted to run it. To her the law was just another business, as Burley would have put it, and couldn't businesses be run in a variety of ways? But she was always practical in facing what she had to cope with, even when it bordered on the irrational.

"I guess you'd better get rid of that young man, and I think I know how to do it. Lose him. In a firm three times your size, would you even notice him?"

"Maybe not, but how do I do that? Are you suggesting a merger?"

"Not I. But Ethelinda's lawyer, Gil Arnheim, is. At least he's been sounding me out. He's beginning to think you're the hottest thing in town. I expect he'd like to grab you while you're still within his range. And, of course, he'd rather join us than fight us over Ethelinda."

I could hardly breathe, as happened to me at moments when my career was suddenly at stake. But my mind, as always at such moments, was cold and clear. I watched her closely.

"Does he want me or my firm?"

"He wants you, but he might take your firm to get you. Would it matter if Mr. Burley got left out in the crunch?"

"No." Nor would it. It wouldn't even matter if Mr. Burley got left in. He became irrelevant. Arnheim & Buttrick was twice our size; joined, we would be one of the major firms of the city. They had big litigation and estates departments, just the fields in which we were weak. The fit was made in heaven! That is, if heaven had anything to do with a man like Gilbert Arnheim. I murmured a silent vow that one of my conditions would be that the new firm should be called Arnheim, Buttrick & Service.

"I think some of my partners might balk at being swallowed up by Gil Arnheim."

"Even if they knew they'd be warm and cozy in his belly?"

"Well, he has a certain reputation. His firm is supposed to be sharp."

"I thought a lawyer couldn't be too sharp."

"There are degrees. They're about the limit."

"You mean they're crooks?"

"No, no, I don't go that far."

"I hardly think Ethelinda would retain a firm of shysters."

"Well, let's put it that Ethelinda likes to win."

"I guess I don't follow you, Bob. You tell me that you're always within the law, just within. You rather brag about it. Isn't that what Gil Arnheim is?"

I considered this. I didn't quite like being bracketed with Arnheim. But wasn't I proposing to make the bracket a real one? I changed the subject.

"If this goes through you ought to get a fat commission. What a wheeler-dealer you are, Sylvia!"

"Oh, don't worry about me. I can look after my compensation. And now that you've finished that drink, my dear, good night."

· 16 ·

GILBERT ARNHEIM and I had a couple of exploratory lunches before we each brought additional partners to more explicit conferences. I found myself liking him. He was short and plump with very thick closely cropped bristling hair and a round, pleasant face with eyes that looked oddly anxious when they were not shiningly reassuring. He was constantly rubbing and folding his hands and assuring me that such and such a thing was "entirely understood"; that it was "easy as pie"; that he'd done it a hundred times. And one felt, too, that he had. There was nothing fake or pretentious about the man. He was what he was.

I was careful, in presenting the proposed merger to my partners, not to evince more than a guarded enthusiasm. I spoke of it at some length at one of our lunches, outlining possible advantages and disadvantages. I pointed out that we witnessed all around us the survival of giants and the decline of dwarfs, that the most successful law firms, like the most successful businesses, were the biggest ones. On the other hand, I anticipated the objections of Oz Burley and his clique by admitting that in such a merger there was bound to be some loss of our personality. I did not feel it necessary to add that that personality was precisely what I wanted to get rid of.

Peter Stubbs surprised me by heading up what I now foresaw would be a minority opposition. He had been present at two of the conferences with Arnheim and had not uttered a word to indicate that he was against the plan.

"I can perfectly see that this merger is going to tempt a lot of you," he said in a tone as moderate as my own. We were all trying to be cool. "And I say at once that I realize that my possession of independent means makes me less vulnerable to that temptation. If our firm should fall apart or go under, I could survive, so the fact that the merger makes us financially sounder is not an inducement to me. I simply don't want to practice law with the sort of men who make up Arnheim & Buttrick. And there isn't much point in my trying to tell you why that is so, because I can't prove a thing against them. Call it a hunch, a smell, an instinct, anything you want. I just don't like them."

This was followed by a general clamor of questions about what it was that Peter didn't like, during which I remained silent. When people have nothing but "hunch" to go on, they will make themselves ridiculous if obliged to talk long enough. A number of the partners, frankly allured by the prospect of greater pay with greater security, became a bit sharp in cross-examining Peter. By the end of our meeting I was reasonably sure that the project had got off to a good start.

Oz Burley confirmed this, walking with me back to the office afterwards, though not in a very flattering fashion.

"Well, I guess you can draw up those merger papers, Bob."

"You think they're really for it?"

"I think *you*'re really for it. And enough of the rest will go along."

"I believe it's the best thing for the firm." I glanced sideways at that arrogant profile. There was not the least hint of anger or resentment in it. "Tell me something, Oz. Why do you dislike me so?"

"I don't dislike you in the least, Bob. I rather admire you, actually, for being so completely what you are. But what you are, you see, is the enemy. I have to fight you. You'll win, of course, but I still have to fight you."

"Oz, what on earth are you talking about? Why am I the enemy? Enemy of what?"

"Oh, there's no point in my going into that," he replied with a laugh that was almost good-natured. "If you could see it, you wouldn't be the enemy. And that's my affair, really. Not yours."

"Well, maybe in the new firm we'll learn to be friends."

"I think if I joined the new firm, that might be possible, even probable. But to avoid it I'll stay clear of the new firm." He chuckled. "Maybe I'd better have a chat with Peter Stubbs. Maybe I can fix up something for myself with him."

He left me to catch up with Peter, who was walking just ahead of us. But shocked though I was by this brief and unpleasant exchange, it was as nothing to what awaited me that night at my meeting with Sylvia.

She had a dinner, as it happened, to which she was not taking me, a new client, and we had agreed that I should come to her apartment for a drink before she had to go out. She was already dressed when I arrived and seemed brimming over with a burden of interesting news.

"Guess what."

"You've got a commission from the pope. The Vatican is raising funds."

"So funny. Listen. Ethelinda's ready to sign that new will."

"Heavens. When?"

"Soon. With that and the merger Sylvia Sands should be able to chant her Nunc Dimittis."

"But isn't it precisely where you are beginning, not ending?"

"Precisely. It is Sylvia Sands who is demitting. It will be Sylvia Service who is commencing."

I was speechless. But had I not known that this was bound to happen? What I think I was most conscious of was that I had never felt farther from Sylvia. "Unfortunately, I'm still married," I at last found breath to say.

"As if I didn't know that. Look, Bob. You're not the

only one who knows the law. Gil Arnheim has given
me the services of a charming young woman lawyer in
his firm who is an expert on domestic relations. She
assures me that from the moment a separation agreement has been signed by you and Alice, she can obtain
a divorce decree for you, binding and valid, within
forty-eight hours."

"But will Alice sign?"

"You know she will. And I know she will. I've talked
to her. She has promised not to stand in our way. The
separation agreement can be drawn tomorrow. Give her
what she wants; her demands are absurdly modest. And
then you and I can be married on Friday!" When I
said nothing, but simply continued to stare at her, I saw
her eyes turn into what I can only describe as fireballs.
"You don't want to? Is that what you're trying to tell
me, Robert Service, that you don't want to? After all
I've done for you? Jesus God, you'd better get out of
here before I kill you!"

"Can't we discuss this rationally?"

"No! And don't imagine that Ethelinda's will can be
signed if we're not married! Or that your merger will
go through if that will isn't signed. Do you think I'm a
total nincompoop? Do you think I'm your slave?"

I know that it is often considered affected and artificial in literary compositions if a character, in a moment
of crisis, compares his situation to that of another character in a remembered novel or play. Yet this often happens to me. Perhaps it is a flaw. Perhaps I should always
be involved, purely and simply, with my own emotions

and those of the person with whom I am in passionate accord or, as now, in passionate disaccord. Anyway, I am not like that. My mind is instantly faced with a parallel or parallels. And at that moment, so help me God, or World Principle, or Soul of the Universe, I thought of the fiery villainess of Racine's tragedy *Bajazet*, the Sultana Roxane, who offers the eponymous hero the choice of death or marriage before she will unleash the army to dethrone his brother and bring him to the crown. But like Bajazet my thoughts went to the gentler Atalide or Alice.

"I'll talk to you tomorrow," I said, rising to go.

"You'll talk to me right now! Jesus, Bob, do you *know* all I've done for you?"

"I'll talk to you tomorrow."

"You're not leaving this apartment, you son of a bitch! You're —"

She had put herself between me and the door, but I thrust her firmly aside, and not waiting for the elevator, hurried down the fire stairs. I heard a loud crash at my feet and looked down to see glass all over the stairs. Sylvia had hurled her glass at my head. Thanking God for her bad aim, I rushed out into the night.

· 17 ·

I THINK I had been as much shocked by Oz's calling
me the "enemy" as by Sylvia's frenzy. I had long been
aware that people might consider me that if they knew
my inner thoughts, but I had also supposed that I should
think the same of them had I known theirs. I had believed
that the dichotomy is so great between what human
beings suppose normal human character to be and what it
actually is that when they chance to perceive the truth
about an individual they jump to the conclusion that he
must be "bad." But what bothered me about Oz's judgment of me was that I had not betrayed my private
thoughts. He had simply deduced them from my acts.

I had a very small opinion, to be sure, of Oz's values,
but the episode recalled unpleasantly to mind two others
in which I had been made to feel a kind of evil presence.
The first went back to my boyhood, when I was twelve,
and it was important, I suppose, mainly because the critic
was my mother, who, in a quarrel between me and her
own mother, had unhesitatingly taken the latter's side.

Grandma Evans, a "gallant" impoverished widow, had made her home with my patient, long-suffering parents. I suppose she had a kind of faded prettiness. Prettiness in an old woman seemed to my adolescent eyes a contradiction in terms, but her silvery, high-piled hair and soft gray eyes and very soft cheeks were agreeable enough. She made a great fuss about "being no trouble" and asking for no special favors; she was always saying that she knew she couldn't live a champagne life on a beer income and that she had been raised, thank God, not to think herself a whit better than anyone else, yet "pesky" headaches and "dratted" colds had a way of entitling her to the "rare treat" of a tray in bed or my afternoon services as a messenger on repeated trips to the drugstore. She was one of those who, when she had a mild seizure or heart attack, maintained with a proud blush that she had been "silly," and she would snort with contempt at anyone who reminded her to take her umbrella or overshoes if the sky threatened rain. Yet these airs, I early suspected, were nothing but the mask of a devouring hypochondria and a crawling fear of death.

It exasperated me that my parents were taken in by this. "Isn't Mother wonderful?" they would exclaim if the old lady consumed a second cocktail that turned her tiddly and even more loquacious than usual. They made an idol of her, and idols, when they are human, are very covetous of worshipers. Grandma had a nostril quick to pick up defection, and she took an early and heartily returned dislike to her only grandson.

Ordinarily my little spars with Grandma ended in a stand-off, but one of them had a more serious finale.

Mother had called out from the kitchen to ask me to go back to the grocer's for an item she had forgotten, and I suppose I had been surly about it. Grandma and I were alone on the porch, she with her knitting, I with my Dumas novel.

"Aren't you going on your errand, Bobby?"

"In due course."

"Your mother said she wanted you to go now."

"I'm going!"

"I don't think you should speak to me in that tone."

"I'm sorry."

"And I suggest when your mother asks you to do something, you should do it more cheerfully."

"Why?"

"Well, you want to show that you recognize all the things she's done for you, don't you? You want to show her that you love her, surely?"

"But she knows that."

"Perhaps she doesn't always know how much."

"I think she knows just how much."

Grandma looked at me critically. "Then perhaps you should try to make her feel that you love her more than you do."

"Wouldn't that be a lie?"

"Hardly a lie, Bobby. Because if you made the effort, you might find that indeed you did love her more."

"Why should I love her more? Isn't it enough the way it is?"

"Love is never enough the way it is. And if I may say so, young man, yours could do with a bit of stretching."

"I bet I love Mummy as much as you do!"

"As *I* do? My own daughter! How dare you say such a thing? What do you know about a mother's love, you fresh young whippersnapper?"

"More than you think. You're always making Mummy wait on you hand and foot. And I've seen you deliberately delay until she was comfortably settled on the sofa before asking her if she'd go upstairs to bring you your shawl."

Grandma at this started to moan and groan as if she were having one of her heart spasms; she clutched at her chest and cried, "Oh, oh, oh!" Of course, she was faking, but self-pitying old hypocrites are capable of working themselves into dangerous states, if for no other reason than to get back at those who have done them an imagined injury. And Grandma certainly had her revenge that day, for Mother came flying out to the porch to help the old lady upstairs to bed, where she remained for twenty-four hours.

Mother waited until Father came home, and they had a conference alone before supper. At that meal Mother delivered an obviously rehearsed homily in a high, sad, hurt tone.

"Your father and I, Bobby, are deeply concerned at your treatment of a defenseless old woman. You chose, deliberately I'm afraid, to strike at her in her most vulnerable area. I cannot conceive where you could have learned such cruelty."

"From her!" I could have shouted back, but I knew it was hopeless. They would never understand. Dimly I realized that my only effective revenge would be silence, and this I rigidly maintained. But I don't think I have forgiven Mother to this day.

The second episode, which occurred when I was seventeen, was much more serious, because here the critic was a person whom I admired. It was Cy Hawkins, or "Mr. Hawkins" as he was always known to me, an English teacher at the Haverstock School in Millbrook, New York, which I attended for one year before matriculating at Columbia. But to preface the tale of my encounter with Mr. Hawkins, I should first give an account of my friendship with Lindsay Knowles.

The Knowleses lived in Keswick, not far from my family, but, oh, the difference. Their great brown multi-winged wooden mansion rambled all over the top of its little hill and was approached by a long macadam drive bordered by rhododendron. I had heard my father say that the criterion of the wealthy was that their houses should not be visible from the road, and I had at once conceived a permanent regard for those whose domiciles met this standard. Our own poor dwelling, of course, looked right out on the street, as did those of most of my high school classmates, but there were some who enjoyed the delectable invisibility, and I identified them enviously with those gateposts in Keswick through which I rarely passed: stone pillars with statues of birds or animals, or silver balls; massive columns supporting heavy opened portals of elaborately wrought iron; simple wooden farm posts, or sometimes simply a break in a well-cut hedge or, at most, two green bushes cut to resemble trees, which my mother, in her unaccountable way, found in "better taste." These estates, or "places," as I learned it was more refined to call them, seemed to me so many Elysian fields at the end of whose graveled drives rose domiciles fit for gods.

Not, I hastily add, that I thought the occupants of these stately homes to be deities. Although grounded in the American obsession with class distinctions, as exemplified in the novels of Fitzgerald, Marquand and O'Hara, and bitterly conscious of every club that might not admit me and every academy with an old-school tie, I still never harbored the smallest admiration for the rich, even the old rich, or the least envy of their superior ease in, say, ordering a meal at an expensive restaurant or acting as master of ceremonies at a bridal dinner. I and my contemporaries wanted what the rich had, but we were perfectly content to keep our manners at all times what they had been. Unlike Gatsby we would not have been impressed by Daisy Buchanan — only by her fortune. Perhaps it was not so much that we were of a later era than that of the three authors mentioned above as that we harked back to an earlier one: Dreiser's.

My parents, who had an exaggerated sense of responsibility for their progenitors and who supported both their mothers into extreme old age, were able to send me to boarding school for only one year, and Haverstock was selected because it was willing to admit boys as late as the twelfth grade. I knew that I would have a tough time there socially, as the boys would have formed all their friendships and cliques, and I resolved, in the summer before going away, to make friends with

Lindsay Knowles, whom I had known in our Keswick public school before he had been sent, three years earlier, to Haverstock. There was no point, after all, in being a "preppie" if one didn't know anyone, and Lindsay, I was sure, would be something of a leader wherever he was.

It was not easy. My parents knew Mr. and Mrs. Knowles, as I knew Lindsay, slightly. His parents asked people like us only to their big Fourth of July lawn parties. But I had early learned a simple thing: that in the absence of some hopeless barrier, such as being black or totally indigent, a dogged persistence will get you almost anywhere. I took to calling Lindsay on the telephone and asking him to play tennis or swim at our little country club, until he decided that, so long as he could see no way out of it, he might as well see me at his place. And once I had made my way past those stone gates it was not difficult to gain a permanent entry. I cultivated Mrs. Knowles, a chatty, fluffy, brainless creature who urged me to "come over and swim" whenever I wanted, which, to Lindsay's barely concealed disgust, I did.

Lindsay was a chameleon; he took on easily the characteristics of any group in which he happened to find himself. He might have been handsome had he weighed twenty pounds less; as it was, he was cheerful and agreeable-looking, with a round, freckled face, long, unruly, sandy hair that fell over his forehead, and gray-blue eyes that could seem merry or ice cold, as his mood required. With boys he could be easygoing, jokey and very lewd; with adults he was apt to be polite with an exaggeration that caused friendly smiles, because it was a conscious exaggeration intended to evoke just such smiles. Alone with an intimate, as I was to learn, he could be moody and bitter. He was exceedingly intelligent but very lazy; he read little but his perfect memory retained every word that he read. His complete ease with people, his sharp tongue and his family's money made him the center of any group of young people in our part of Keswick.

My selection of Lindsay as a friend-to-be was not motivated entirely by his being an "old boy" at Haverstock. There were two other youths in Keswick who also attended that institution and to whom access would have been more facile. But I had discovered something about Lindsay that only he, his parents and his doctor knew: that he was afflicted with a serious heart ailment. I had learned this in a part-time summer job with the Knowleses' doctor, a great friend of my parents, who had entrusted me with the task of reorganizing his voluminous files according to a new system and putting aside for proposed destruction certain antiquated ones. It was thus that I happened upon his memorandum of Lindsay's case, in which it was set forth that the boy should be told of the gravity of his condition in order to ensure his compliance with the regimen laid down. The prognosis was not wholly negative. It was possible, if not probable, that his condition would improve. It was thought best that he should continue his normal schedule at home and at school, while avoiding certain physical exercises.

If Lindsay had not revealed to any of his friends the threat under which he lived — and I have a hunch that he was too proud to have done so — would he not relish a friend who, without himself being aware of the illness, offered him a sympathy, when the dark moods fell, that could not be connected with an odious pity? And might that not prove my open sesame at boarding school?

Lindsay was inclined to resent my ready acceptance of his mother's casual invitations, but the summer was long and hot, and the Knowleses did not leave Keswick — no doubt with the purpose of keeping their son quiet. There were times, therefore, when I found him alone, sunbathing by the pool, and, for all his desire to snub me, glad enough to have a companion. On my third visit we became almost friendly.

"Why do you come here, Bob?" he asked. "You can't think I've been very nice to you."

"You've got a king-size pool and an all-weather tennis court. So I take your snottiness as a kind of dues I have to pay."

"Don't you know other people with pools and courts?"

"Pools, yes. Courts, no. And no one I know has a pool this big. It's great to do lengths in."

Lindsay looked at me now with something like interest. "Well, I'll say this for you. You put your cards on the table."

"Isn't that where cards belong?"

"Why are you going to Haverstock, Bob?"

"Isn't it a good school?"

"It's all right, I suppose, as such academies go. But it's no better than Keswick High."

"You mean you get nothing for all that tuition?"

"Not really. What the prep schools are good at is bringing along the dumb guys. They have enough faculty to give individual tutoring. But now they won't take the dumb guys. So what's the use of them?"

I knew better than to tell him that there might be social advantages for me in going to a prep school. He was sure to sneer at that. "I guess my old man's pretty keen on having me go. Personally, I think the bright guys teach themselves. Give 'em the books; they'll read."

"And you're a bright guy?"

"I am. Aren't you?"

"Maybe I am at that." He appeared to consider this, almost gravely. "Anyway, what does it matter? The bomb should take care of us all."

Was he trying to console himself by including the world in his own doom? "I figure nothing ever happens that everyone thinks will happen," I observed sententiously.

"So you believe the world will survive to become Robert Service's oyster?"

"And Lindsay Knowles's. I'll share it with you."

"Because of my pool?"

"Because of your father's pool."

"Actually, I believe the place is in Mummy's name." He laughed. "And, come to think of it, there is a master at Haverstock who might teach you more than you can get out of a book. It's Mr. Hawkins."

"What's he like?"

"Well, you'll see. He's not like the others. He's somehow . . . real." Lindsay became suddenly self-conscious. "He makes poetry seem something more than a lesson, or a thing to quote and impress people with. It's like religion to him. Except a religion you really believe in, not just Sunday stuff. Oh, I don't know. It's a lot of crap, of course."

And that was all I could get out of him about Mr. Hawkins. But it was a start, anyway, for after that Lindsay greeted me with a more resigned good will when I appeared, and once, on a rainy afternoon, actually telephoned me to ask me over to play backgammon.

He was certainly unhappy. He would sometimes be silent for minutes on end, not even acknowledging a direct question. This might be followed by ribald moods in which he would giggle inanely at anything that was said. At other times he could be sour, critical, even corrosive. He would say scathing things to me and did not seem to note that I never answered back. He appeared to have accepted me as a hanger-on whom it was not worth taking the trouble to be rid of, perhaps as a kind of courtier. For there was something oddly imperial about Lindsay. He took for granted that he should be an object of some kind of deference, not so much because of his money (his family was only rich by Keswick standards) or his brain (which was no better than mine), but perhaps simply because he had been dignified by the probability of an early demise.

Haverstock School was a medley of rather dull,

oblong, red-brick buildings spread out over a long low hilltop with a superb view of the rolling verdant landscape of upper New York. I entered a form of some fifty boys and found that, as I had anticipated, Lindsay's support was a valuable social asset. But there were liabilities to it as well. In one mood he might include me in a hiking expedition across country with one or two of the school leaders, but in another he would make cruel public fun of me and imply that he had to be nice to me only because I was from his home town.

He did, however, make me part of his relationship with Mr. Hawkins, and he and I would go to the latter's study on Saturday evenings to drink cider and talk of poetry.

The English teacher was a large man with beautiful wide friendly eyes, a very pale countenance and thick red curly hair. Motionless he might have seemed the statue of a Greek discus thrower. But his actions and demeanor seemed to deprecate the outer man, not from any sense that his exterior might be too shining a coat of armor for the soul cringing within (the initial interpretation of some observers) as from a deep and almost desperate sense of genuine humility. Cy Hawkins, one felt, would be ready, if not to fight, certainly to die — and die in flames — for a cause, but it would be difficult for him to believe that any enemy or condemning judge could be more sinful than he.

His religious faith, unlike any that I had observed at home, was ardent. How far it went was revealed in a discussion that he and I and Lindsay had one Saturday night about Gerard Manley Hopkins's "The Wreck of the *Deutschland*." Mr. Hawkins read aloud the stanzas in which the tall nun, facing imminent death as the tumultuous sea pounded over the deck of the stranded vessel, calls out, "O Christ, O Christ, come quickly!" He read this with a passion that almost choked him, and then broke off to explain his belief that there had been an actual appearance of Christ in that stormy sky.

"You mean that he really appeared, or that Hopkins is inventing it?" I asked.

"Both, perhaps."

"Then why didn't the other people see him?"

"How do you know they didn't?"

"The survivors would have told, wouldn't they?"

"Maybe he appeared only to the tall nun," Lindsay suggested. "Wasn't that common with visitations?"

"Or maybe only the pure in heart could see him," I added.

"I don't know," Mr. Hawkins responded gravely. "It seems to me that he must have been visible to all who looked. What an ineffable experience!"

"A rather cold and damp one."

"Not to say fatal," Lindsay added.

"But that is not the way Hopkins saw it," Mr. Hawkins protested. "He believed that God sends terrible deaths to those he most loves. He held that suffering was an honor, and martyrdom the greatest of all. The early Christians seem to have felt that way, too. There is evidence that they marched into the arena joyfully."

"And Hitler's holocaust, was that a blessing?" I demanded.

"You could argue it," Mr. Hawkins replied sturdily. "For its victims anyway. The diary of Anne Frank has elements of sainthood in it."

"Can a Jew be a saint?" Lindsay asked.

"Why not? God is not an Episcopalian. Nor even a Catholic."

"But if persecution is a blessing," I pursued, "must not the persecutors be benefactors?"

" 'It must needs be that offenses come, but woe to that man by whom the offense cometh!' "

"So the Nazis will go to hell?"

"If you believe there is such a place, Bob. If ever I am tempted to become a Catholic, it will be because they have learned to face the vilest in human nature. It doesn't shock them, and it shouldn't shock them. It's simply truth. God's truth."

"But surely the Nazis were worse?"

"Than whom? Us? Which life would you choose, Bob? A Berlin physician, brilliant and recognized, who is gassed with his wife and children at Auschwitz, aged thirty-five, or a black in our old South who dies in peace, illiterate, surrounded by his children and grandchildren, at eighty?"

"The doctor, of course."

"I thought so. What thinking man would not prefer death to enforced darkness? Where cruelty is concerned, there's not much to choose between humans."

It is difficult for me to describe the peculiar excitement

that Mr. Hawkins's thinking gave me. And yet I was not, oddly enough, even much attracted by his faith. I did not imagine that the God in whom he believed with such passion would preserve his throbbing soul after death any more than he would Adolf Hitler's. But it thrilled me to be in contact with a man so devoid of sham who believed, in perfect simplicity, that a hideous and cruel death might be a blessing, not even in disguise. It was as if Mr. Hawkins had somehow got the better of a coldly mechanical universe; he was a hot, bright little coal lying on a desert of rock, doomed to go out but shining bravely while it could.

As the year progressed, Lindsay became more extreme in all his attitudes. With those who talked smut he was smuttier; with snobs he was snobbier, and he continued to be sharp and critical with me when we were in the company of other boys. Yet he would seek my company for solitary weekend walks to the river, never apologizing for his earlier treatment. He was one of those who could divide his life into unconnecting departments. If he wanted to be an aristocrat on Monday, or a jokester on Tuesday, he saw no reason why that should keep him from being a poet or philosopher on Saturday.

I particularly remember a talk that we had one Sunday in April. Lindsay now tired very easily, so instead of taking our usual walk we had climbed to the top of the chapel tower and stood looking out on the panorama of the countryside and the diminished school.

"I suppose Mr. Hawkins would think that now we're closer to heaven."

"I think he finds heaven everywhere," I responded.

"He is fortunate."

"A fortunate fool?"

"If that's what a believer is."

"Would you like to be one?"

"And a fool? Why not? But sometimes I think heaven is only for older people. That they've had time to earn it. That it couldn't be for someone our age. Does it seem likely that a baby could have an afterlife?"

The subject was spooky to me; I changed it. "Why do you only like me when we're just the two of us together, Lindsay?"

He laughed. "What makes you think I do then?"

"Because you act so differently. Sometimes, in a gang, you seem ashamed of me."

"I'm not. It's just that I find it easier to say the things people expect. Just as it's easier to wear the things they wear. None of it means anything. But with Mr. Hawkins — and with you at times, when you're not showing off about something you've read — I can almost think. Or kid myself that I'm thinking."

I was divided between pique and pleasure. Did I really show off? And then I felt a sudden shock of pity. Lindsay seemed remote as he stared at the hills to the west. He looked older and puffier.

"What do you want to think about?" I asked.

"Oh, anything!"

I felt constrained. I had no idea what he needed. I racked my brain for a subject. "Do you think Hopkins would have been a better poet if he hadn't been a Jesuit?"

"I don't know and care less," he snapped, turning on me impatiently. "The trouble with you, Service, is that you're an atheist who's trying to create a deity. You should beware of graven images. You want to throw away Hopkins's God and deify his poetry. You're like all those tourists in Europe squinnying at stained glass windows and holy statues and religious paintings and yacking about 'tactile values' or 'significant form,' as if God had had nothing to do with all that art. Well, maybe he hadn't. But what's the point of it all if he didn't? God, if God there be, must despise people like you!"

"And what about people like you?"

"Oh, I'm out of it. Or will be soon."

Poor boy, he was. He had a bad attack the very next week and had to be taken out of school. He did not write, but his parents informed the headmaster that he was going to Arizona for a better climate and would not be coming back to Haverstock.

Mr. Hawkins seemed much upset by Lindsay's departure; he had had no previous suspicion of a grave illness. I suppose he asked himself if he should not have given more time to the unfortunate lad, and he made himself freely available to me, perhaps to ensure that he should at least have done his duty by me should I too come down with a complaint of angina. That may sound silly, but it was the kind of man Mr. Hawkins was. I took full advantage of his kindness, realizing that this was a greater academic opportunity than any other offered by the school.

One Saturday afternoon we hiked many miles across

the meadows, climbed a little hill and paused on the summit to recline and take in the exquisite sylvan scene. Mr. Hawkins seemed unusually exhilarated, and he intoned solemnly the great lines from *Tintern Abbey*:

> "And I have felt
> A presence that disturbs me with the joy
> Of elevated thoughts; a sense sublime
> Of something far more deeply interfused,
> Whose dwelling is the light of setting suns,
> And the round ocean and the living air,
> And the blue sky, and in the mind of man."

"Do you think Wordsworth would have felt that here?" I asked.

"Of course. Don't you?"

"Well, I was wondering to what extent his emotion had been activated by a particular landscape. You think any landscape would have done the trick?"

"Any beautiful one, yes."

"But what about his 'Poor Susan'? She was standing inhaling the vapors of Cheapside, and it's an equally beautiful poem."

Mr. Hawkins looked perplexed. "But it's not a poem about the direct impact of nature. Susan is *remembering* the delights of the countryside that she has lost."

"So that's it. It's all in the mind, in memory, is it? Wordsworth could have had his elevated thoughts anywhere, so long as he'd seen one landscape. Or did he really need one? Couldn't he imagine it?"

Mr. Hawkins frowned; he wanted to enjoy the panorama before him. "I suppose so," he murmured.

"It would be a good subject for an essay, wouldn't it? Do you think it would do for my end-of-term paper?"

He reached over at this to give me a friendly admonitory pat. "Must you always be thinking of what you're going to write about something, Bob? Can't you just give yourself to an experience like this? Can't you simply enjoy it?"

"But isn't that enjoying it?"

"Not really. Do you know, Bob, it sometimes occurs to me — now don't be offended — that you are 'putting on' literature, as if it were some kind of tool or weapon that would be useful to you in the battle of life."

"And it isn't?"

"Well, it might be, I suppose. But its real use is subjective. It's for your private edification."

"I don't see the difference. What edifies privately must be of some ultimate practical use."

"Let me put it this way. Suppose yourself marooned on a Pacific island. There is delectable fruit and beautiful native girls — call it a veritable paradise on earth — but there is no chance to satisfy worldly ambition and nobody with whom you can discuss literature. Would you read as eagerly as you do now?"

"I suppose a lot of the point would be gone if I couldn't talk about it."

"Yet Wordsworth would be just as fine."

"Look here, Mr. Hawkins." I extracted from my pocket a paperback copy of *The Prelude*. "Wordsworth doesn't agree with you. In the very beginning of *The Prelude* he says that enjoying nature without writing about it is acting 'like a peasant.' " I opened the book and searched until I found this passage, which I read triumphantly to him. For, of course, I had prepared myself for the encounter.

> "I had hopes
> Still higher, that with a frame of outward life
> I might endue, might fix in a visible home
> Some portion of those phantoms of conceit."

Mr. Hawkins chuckled as he conceded my point. "Very good. But that is the poet speaking. Wordsworth felt it his duty to put his thoughts in verse for our edification. But that doesn't mean that you and I have to write. He gives his verse to us out of his bounty. We need simply enjoy it."

"But he gets all the glory!" I exclaimed.

Mr. Hawkins laughed, but did not reply. I loved that hour with him. I felt an openness in his nature that I had never experienced in another human being. I felt that at last I was in the company of a man who would understand me because he understood himself, because he had a sane conception of the value of human character. Had he not said that Catholics accepted the universe?

"And isn't everything we think and do a part of our organized life?" I continued. "Is it really possible to isolate any experience? Would there be a sound in a forest when a tree fell if there was no ear to hear? Suppose that I read a beautiful poem. It enters my mind and imagination. It contributes to my education and culture. An educated and cultivated man makes a greater mark in his community. Doesn't that give the poem a greater role than simply being read on a beach on that Pacific island of yours?"

"Are you really such a utilitarian, Bob? Do you apply your doctrine to everything in life?"

"*I* don't apply it. It's there."

"In everything? At home, in school? In friendship?" He paused, and there was a hint of something more serious in those kindly eyes, perhaps a hope that I would deny his suspicion, or at least a fear that he might be going too far, that he might be on the verge of discovering too much about me. "You've been a very good friend to Lindsay. You never resented his mean remarks. I admired that in you."

"Well, I knew he was sick."

"Did you? Oh, of course, you're both from Keswick, aren't you? I suppose your families knew."

"My family didn't. I found out about it in his doctor's office."

As I related the circumstances of my discovery Mr. Hawkins remained totally still and silent. I should have been warned by this, but I wasn't. I plunged on blindly. At last he interrupted with an interpretation of my tale that he seemed to be almost begging me to accept.

"I see it, Bob. You realized that poor Lindsay was in for a bad time and that he was going to need a patient and sympathetic friend."

"That was part of it. But I was also going to need a friend at Haverstock. It was what biologists call a case of symbiosis."

"Did you ever tell him you knew?"

"Oh, no. He would have rejected pity. I knew what I was doing."

"I see."

And then *I* saw, too. He was appalled. I had been a fool to think I had found a man who could face the truth. Mr. Hawkins, like the rest of them, wanted to live in a world of make-believe.

"You think I'm horrible!"

"I don't think any such thing." He scrambled to his feet. "I think you're a sensible young man with a good head on your shoulders. I think you'll go very far. But I wonder a bit if writing is the career for you. I think I see you in something . . . more active. Well, shall we be getting back?"

My vague dreams of being a writer were probably quelled at this point, though they persisted into Columbia. Mr. Hawkins remained on friendly terms with me for my last weeks at school, but we were less intimate now. This was my fault. His Christian heart embraced me even with my disclosed flaw, but I did not care to receive the benefit of his charity. I did not regard what I had disclosed as a flaw. I had learned another lesson in the dangers of self-revelation. Henceforth I would keep my soul to myself.

That summer, after graduation, when I went over to see Lindsay, who had returned from Arizona, I was told he was too ill to have any visitors. But his father came down to the front hall to talk to me. Mr. Knowles had always been in the city working on the days that I had come to swim at his place, and I knew him only by sight. He did not know me at all, but his air was cordial.

"So you're Bobby Service. Lindsay has told me some fine things about you. That you had only one year at Haverstock and helped him to learn more than in the other three. And that you've read all of *The Ring and the Book* and *The Faerie Queene*. If you become a lawyer like your old man, you're going to be the most literary one since Francis Bacon. And didn't he write all of Shakespeare, too?"

Mr. Knowles was the finest type of Yankee aristocrat, if that's not an oxymoron, a plain old shoe of a man, with short grizzled gray hair and leathery cheeks, a high-pitched laugh and the kindest, gentlest eyes I have ever seen.

"Let me tell you something, Bob," he said as he took me to the door. "You're going to have the life my boy may not have. Always remember that's a reason for you to be sure to get an extra kick out of every minute of it!"

I'm afraid that what I most minded when Lindsay died, only a month later, was that I could not see Mr. Knowles again. There was simply no way that he and I could be friends. It made Keswick and my parents seem duller than ever.

As a freshman at Columbia that fall I began at last seriously to brace myself for the future. I think I always had known, deep down, that I was not going to be a writer. I had too worldly a nature to cope with. But I still had my college years in which to equip myself with a philosophy that would carry me through at least the early years of my professional life — assuming, as I largely did, that I should be a lawyer. I had just about totally destroyed the last remnants of the parental standards and made a clean sweep of the lares and penates above their hearth. I was like Marius, whose "only possible dilemma lay between that old ancestral religion, now become so incredible to him, and the honest action of his own untroubled, unassisted intelligence."

And it was at just this point that not only my intelligence but my heart was confronted with the greatest exception I have ever known to my category of "shams." I fell in love with Alice.

· 18 ·

It was amazing how totally that hurled glass cured
me of Sylvia. I was as cold to her now as some keeper
of a zoo of big cats who, thinking he has made friends
with one of the glowing tawny animals, enters her cage
to find himself savagely scratched and gored. Obviously,
that is the nature of the beast, and the keeper has no one
to blame but his careless self. I recognized that Sylvia's
very fury may have been evidence of her attachment
to me, even of her passion, but it was equally a fact that
I cannot value affection expressed so violently — nay,
I actually abhor it. All I wanted to do was slam shut the
door of her cage and walk away from that zoo for all
time.

But I must say this for Sylvia. She knew when something was over. She made no desperate midnight calls
to me, nor did I find any message on my desk the following morning. That shattered glass was an effective
farewell.

I felt a strange stupor. I did not even look at my mail. I had no concern for Ethelinda's will or for the great merger that had been the subject of so many conferences. Was I a monster to have so little feeling for people who had done so much for me? Well, so be it. I didn't care. I was what I was.

My secretary entered, in response to my buzz. She was a silent, efficient, dark-complexioned middle-aged woman who never made personal remarks, worked any number of hours that I requested and had, I fatuously assumed, a crush on me.

"I'm going away, Elaine." The news came almost as much of a surprise to myself as to her. "I'm going away for a few days, and I shall leave no forwarding address. I shan't be reachable to anyone."

"And the merger?"

"The merger can take care of itself."

"What about your family, Mr. Service? What shall I do if one of the girls is ill?"

"Their mother can take care of that."

"If you will allow me to say, Mr. Service —"

"No, Elaine, I will not allow you to say anything. Just put it down that I'm temporarily off my rocker. Don't worry. I'll get back on it again."

I strode quickly down the corridor and out of the office, ignoring the receptionist's cry, "Lunch, Mr. Service?"

I went home, packed a bag, got my car from the garage and drove north to Millbrook. I found the little inn where my parents had stayed at the time of my graduation from Haverstock School; it was still in busi-

ness and I took a room. Later that evening I drove to
the school and called on Mr. Hawkins.

He was alone in his study, correcting examination
papers, but he jumped up to greet me with a heart-
warming welcome. I had seen him only half a dozen
times in the eighteen years since my graduation, and he
had changed very little, except that he was stouter and
his hair, prematurely for one still under sixty, was now
a snowy white. He was still a bachelor, and as intense
and benevolent as ever. He let me talk until late that
night as if he had nothing else to do, and the following
afternoon we went for a ramble in the autumnal woods.

"I have thought of you often through the years, Bob.
I wondered what was ultimately going to happen to
you." Hawkins paused here to fix those glowing, concerned eyes on me. "I was terribly afraid it was going
to be something bad."

"Like this?"

"Well, of course, I didn't know what form it would
take. What I feared was that when you got what you
wanted — and I was always sure you were going to get
that — you would find it turn to dust and ashes in your
mouth."

"Doesn't it for everybody?"

"Oh, my, no. Lots of people are utterly content with
the rewards of this world. But you had been vouchsafed
a vision of better things. You had loved Wordsworth
and Hopkins. You knew long passages of *The Prelude*
by heart. How were you ever going to be satisfied in
a shallow pond?"

"But you never believed that I cared for Wordsworth!" I remonstrated, half indignant that his memory should be so flattering. "You thought I was a fraud, a phony! That I only read to get good marks and show off!"

"Is that what you thought I thought?" he asked in distress. "Is that what you think other people think?"

"It's what I know they think."

"My dear Bob, I may not have done you a good turn in encouraging your love of letters. Of course, I always knew there was a worldly side to your cultivation of the fruit of that garden. But that's not as uncommon as you seem to think. What I may have failed to recognize was that you were mixing two incompatible things: a *real* love of beauty with a *real* love of success. And perhaps that hasn't been possible since the Renaissance. Why don't you go back to your wife? She, I gather, at least shares your literary tastes. That's better than Mrs. Sands, surely."

"Alice won't have me."

"She wouldn't have the man you were yesterday. She might have the man you are today."

I seized on the idea at once. I knew now that I had been waiting for him to say it, that I had come up to Millbrook to hear him say it. "She's my soul," I murmured, and I was afraid that I sounded greedy.

"Maybe you're still a little bit hers."

I drove down to Keswick in the late afternoon and found Mother alone. Father was off on a fishing trip, but she was willing to give me supper and put me up for the night. We sat up late while I told her my story.

She listened with that cool, faintly disapproving but essentially resigned air that she so often adopted with me.

"So you'll go back to Alice now? What will she say, do you think?"

"That's what I want you to tell me. You see her more than I do. Has she got anyone else?"

"One of her poets, maybe. I don't know how much there is in it. I met him once there. A John Cross. He's middle-aged, rather small and quiet, and walks with a limp. I believe he had infantile as a child."

"He doesn't sound like a very formidable rival."

"Don't be too sure. He may give Alice something she needs. Something you didn't give her. Are you really sure, Robert, that you want to go back to her?" Mother's eyes seemed to search me as if I had just reconfirmed that I should always be an enigma to her.

"Of course I'm sure!"

"Because I think she may be on the way to finding some kind of peace in her life. I'd hate to have her all riled up again."

Mother had never learned that the most essential maternal quality is loyalty — loyalty that can be blind, if necessary. The failure of this quality in a mother does even more damage than its presence does good. I felt at that moment that Mother was simply responsible for all the bad things in my life.

"I think I'll mix myself a stiff drink and take it to bed," I muttered in a kind of growl.

The next day was Saturday, and I found Alice at

home when I telephoned. The girls were both at friends' houses for the weekend; she agreed, when I told her it was important, to see me any time that I wanted to call. I arrived at the apartment that evening at five to find her reading manuscripts by a fire. For the third time in two days I related the events of the preceding week. I told her that the revision of the Low will had upset our merger plans and that my old firm would now continue as it had been. I knew this to be a point in my favor as Alice, kept up to date in such matters by her good friends, the Peter Stubbses, did not like the prospect of Gil Arnheim.

"You see me right back where you and I started," I concluded. "I believe that I'm perfectly capable of doing as well as I did before, although it will be a handicap to have the record of a split-off merger to live down. But that, however, will be as nothing if I could have you with me again."

Our eyes met in a long stare. She was startled because she had not expected this ending. I was startled because she looked tired and even a bit older. I had been idealizing her for two stunned days; I had built up a high vision of pale, lofty beauty. But I quickly recovered. I loved Alice. I adored Alice. And I still do. We are all subject to these devastating and disillusioning flashes. It is part of learning to live to become indifferent to them.

"Oh, Bob, do you really mean that?" There was nothing in her tone that offered me the smallest encouragement.

"I mean that and much more. In the future you would

be my guide in all ethical questions involved in my practice."

"But I don't ask for that. I don't want it!"

"*I* ask for it. Because I need it. I want to put our marriage back together on a basis that will wholly satisfy you. I have never stopped loving you. Sylvia was an interlude, one of those things that happen to lonely men. Why can't you and I be together and bring up our daughters as they should be brought up? If you're worried about love, you needn't be. You can have a separate bedroom for as long as you like. Of course, I'd always hope that would end, but it would be only a hope."

"I know I should think of the children," she said, turning her face from me. "But I have to think of myself, too. You say Sylvia was an interlude. I'm not at all sure I want to call my friend John that."

What a thing is jealousy! In a second the wan and tired look had disappeared from her countenance. Alice was as beautiful as when I had first loved her!

"Are you in love with him?" I cried.

Had Alice lit a fire in the grate so that she could stare into it? It seemed a necessary prop to her thoughtful reflection.

"No, I won't say I'm in love with John. I've wanted to be, I think. He's a wonderful man, and we've been very comfortable together. I never believed you'd come back like this. I thought you'd go from glory to glory."

"Not what you'd consider glory."

"Perhaps not. But I had a suspicion that without me

to nag you you might develop more naturally. That you'd become a —"

"A tycoon?"

"I suppose so. Anyway, I don't think I'm quite prepared for this new Bob Service."

"You prefer me the other way?"

"No, no, it's not that." She shrugged uneasily. "It's just as I say, that I'm not ready."

"You don't trust my conversion?"

"I don't *know*, Bob!" she exclaimed, shaking her head in sudden pique. "I had told myself that I had been too prim and fussy. That, after all, you had never done anything actually wrong. That the world was a hundred times more your world than it was mine. That I had better face a few facts. And then I thought that if I was humble it would be all right for me to live alone with my own standards and ideas. And perhaps one day with John and his."

"I'll do all I can to prevent it!" I cried. "It means everything to me to have another chance with you. Even if I have to appeal to your sense of duty and what you owe the children."

"Oh, don't!"

"Because it wouldn't work?"

"No, because it might."

I paused for a second, suppressing something like a sob. "Do you dislike me so much?"

"No, no. In fact, I've never really gotten you out of my system. That's what to some extent has blocked me with John. But how can I go back to that former life, knowing it's only a matter of time before the old Bob reasserts himself?" She turned from the little flame with a kind of desperation in her eyes. "Why must I go through all this torment again?"

"Because this time it's going to be different."

"I'm sure you believe that. But can't you see it's hard for me to?"

"Yes."

Alice allowed me to take her out for dinner, and, away from the too haunting and familiar scene of our old apartment, in the green coolness and elegance of the Amboise, she relaxed and drank three cocktails in fairly rapid succession.

"Haven't you rather stepped up your quota?" I inquired, as she ordered the last one.

"No. In fact, I'd almost given them up. I'm afraid of solitary drinking. But tonight is exceptional, and I'm behaving exceptionally."

We talked about the girls at considerable length; we talked about her parents and mine; we even talked about Sylvia, and, finally, about John Cross.

"I am going to go to see him tomorrow," I announced.

"John? My God, why?"

"I'm going to present my case to him. You tell me he is a man of honor, of sensitivity. Well, I plan to approach him as such. I shall bare my life to him. I shall even give him some pages of my journal to read, about you and me. I shall propose that he decide whether he thinks I have the right to ask you to come back to me."

Alice stared as if I had presented her with a new and utterly unexpected side of Robert Service.

"Poor John! Would you really put him through that?"

"Why not? When I took up with Sylvia I left you free. He had every right to enter your life. It is only fair that I should advise him that I intend to evict him if I can."

"You sound so legal. What do you suppose John's and my relationship to be?"

"I don't even want to ask. All I know is that he has acquired a place in your confidence that is a substitute for mine."

Alice brooded about this for a moment. "Well, he's certainly heard enough about you," she said at last. "He'll probably be fascinated to meet you. And, of course, as a writer he'll want to burrow his nose into that famous journal. He works as a consultant to Scribner's. You may even get a contract offer!"

Alice was certainly in a funny mood that night. She drank a good deal of wine, in addition to her cocktails, and talked to me about her authors, something which she had never done in the past. I began to have hopes as to how the evening might terminate.

And indeed I ended, as I should have, back in my wife's bed. But there was something different about it. Alice was less personal, more interested in the act than the lover. She even seemed a bit desperate in her need for it; she acted like a woman long deprived. Although she was not quite the Alice I remembered and longed to have back, I derived consolation from the thought that she had probably not been sleeping with Cross.

In the morning, however, when I asked if I could now move my things back to the apartment, she shook her head.

"Not yet, dear. Not quite yet."

· 19 ·

JOHN CROSS looked at me in our booth in the New Galway Bar as if I were some uncanny animal that would probably behave itself but that just might spit or strike. He had a Scotch and soda that he nursed while I consumed three. I was nervous and did not care if I showed it. He was a small, rather dumpy man with a strangely boyish face for his at least forty years and small, twinkling, sympathetic dark eyes under a high brow and a shock of black hair. I say that his eyes were "sympathetic" because they struck me as being so, even to myself. Cross's self-confidence, I deduced, must have been based on some estimate of his own good character; it could hardly have drawn much support from his bodily physique or worldly success. But I could see why Alice liked him, and this made me tense.

"What we both should be thinking of is Alice," I said firmly. "That is, what is best for her."

"You mean which of us is best for her."

"All right, that's a good way to put it."

"Only I'm not sure it is. Am I really entitled to put it that way? Alice has never said she would consider marrying me, even if she were free. And, regardless of what you may suspect, we have not been lovers."

"Really?" My heart was like that singing bird Alice and I used to quote. "I assume that is not because you have not suggested it."

"Oh, no. I have been bold enough to offer even so poor a thing as myself. You can't object to that, can you?" His smile presumed my agreement, but a small gleam in his eye betrayed that he was still aware of the unpredictable beast before him. "I love Alice. I make no bones about that. But I tell you frankly that she does not return my love. I think perhaps she would like to, but, there you are, she doesn't."

"Why do you suppose she doesn't?"

"I'm afraid that's your fault, old boy. She hasn't been able to dispose of her feeling for you."

"John, I have subjected you to the tedium of reading my journal for nothing!" I exclaimed. "I apologize."

"Why do you say that?"

"Isn't it obvious? If Alice still loves me and doesn't love you, you're too much of a gentleman to remain in the lists."

"You are quite wrong, my friend. It is just what I might do. And it may be that I have not read those engrossing yellow pages that you left with my doorman this morning in vain. For the question is more than ever a valid one: which of us is the better man for Alice?"

"But if she doesn't love you, John!"

"Love isn't everything. The question is what your love — if that's the right word for it — will do to Alice. Consider what it's already done to her."

"What?"

John was silent for a moment, as if debating how much a jungle cat could take. "I don't suppose you asked me here tonight to talk in platitudes. Very well, then, here goes. You have driven her to the verge of a kind of moral bankruptcy. Year after year she has watched you, like one hypnotized, stalking your goals relentlessly. And she's never once been able to convince you that you were wrong!"

"Doesn't that suggest I was not?"

"Yes! That is precisely what it does. And that's what she has found so difficult to live with. The idea that it was, after all, your world and not hers."

"And couldn't it be?"

"No!" John's now fiery eyes challenged me to strike if I wanted. "It cannot be like that! You are wrong, Robert Service, just as wrong as you can be. The man in your journal — he can't totally be you, can he? — is a kind of monster. What do you really want Alice for? What do you really need her for? Is she some kind of hostage to take with you through life so that the angels dare not strike you down?"

I suppose at this point I became a bit hysterical, for I don't recall with just what words I formed my answer. I am sure I told him that I had loved Alice since our college days, that she was both the rudder and the anchor of my life, that I felt exposed and hideously vulnerable without her, that I really did not know how I should live if I could not get her back. I must have ranted on for fifteen minutes.

"I imagine she keeps you from seeing yourself," I remember his retorting bitterly in the end. "But why in the name of all that's holy do you insist on keeping that terrible journal?"

"I'll give it up if you'll give her back!" I cried. "I'll let *her* be my journal!"

In the end poor John himself seemed about to collapse. He ordered a double Scotch and drank it neat.

"I'm beginning to wonder what I'm doing in all this," he muttered glumly. "You and Alice. Talk about two scorpions in a bottle! It's all very well to ask what's best for her, but what about what's best for *you*? Suppose you're a damned soul that only she can save? If she took the job on, perhaps she ought to finish it. As long, anyway, as she doesn't want to take *me* on."

After we had walked, rather unsteadily, at least on my part, back to my building, I asked John if he would try to persuade Alice to let me come back.

"No, I won't do that," he responded wearily. "But I'll certainly leave her alone. To make up her own mind."

And with that he left me.

· 20 ·

AT MY OFFICE on Monday morning I found a desk covered with angry pink telephone slips, a secretary torn between indignation and relief at the sight of me and my exasperated partner Douglas, alerted to my arrival by the receptionist, looming in the doorway with expectant, probing eyes. But his first announcement forestalled further questions and explanations.

"A Mrs. Ethelinda Low has been on my telephone since nine o'clock, Bob. She wants you to go to her at once. She says it's a matter of life and death."

With hardly another word I left the office. Twenty minutes later I was seated with Ethelinda in her library before the bust of the Pompadour. Ethelinda was in a sorry state of nerves.

"I don't know where to turn, Robert, or whom to trust. I don't even know if I can trust you. But there's something in your face that always makes me think I can. Or is it only that Sylvia has been badmouthing you so? Oh, Robert, it's all too terrible. Gil Arnheim says that girl has been trying to get her hands on my estate. He claims she's been a designing minx from the very beginning. And I, who thought I knew what such people were! I, to fall for an old ruse like that!"

I made mental note of the fact that when the aged begin to deteriorate, even the strong aged, they go fast. This intrepid woman had seemed an impregnable fort, her drawbridge raised, her gates bolted, her standard proudly flying, her machicolated battlements manned by archers. And now, suddenly, the enemy was over the walls, in the courtyard, despoiling the corpses of her guard. She had been betrayed from within, alone and helpless in a world of plunderers.

"Why does Gil suddenly think that Sylvia is mercenary?" I asked.

"Because he says that the idea of the charitable trust was all hers. That she wasn't crude enough or obvious enough to ask me for a direct bequest. That what she wanted was the power of running the trust and paying herself huge commissions in the Surrogate's Court."

"But surely he was drafting your will. Why didn't he suggest that you use a foundation instead of a trust?"

"He says that until last week he had taken for granted that I knew exactly what I wanted. And that there was nothing innately wrong with the idea of a charitable trust. But when he found out it was Sylvia's idea . . . Oh, Robert, help me — I don't know whom to believe!"

As always in a crisis I thought fast. Gil must have realized, as soon as Sylvia had told him of our breach, that he would have to choose between us. He must have then quickly weighed the value to him of the merger of our firms as opposed to an alliance with an angry and frustrated female public relations officer. The choice, once made, was followed immediately by the decision to destroy Sylvia in his client's eyes. Gil, quite sensibly, would hang on to Ethelinda and me. Who could blame him?

"Here is what I advise you to do, Ethelinda," I said firmly. "Set up your foundation. Now. Right away. Put on its board of governors half a dozen men and women of known public spirit and character, and of independent means. Provide that they will serve at nominal compensation, but with a salaried director and staff. Then give them some money and see how they do with it. If the thing works, you can leave your estate to it. Otherwise you can go back to your old idea of leaving it outright to charity."

"Oh, Robert, that sounds so sensible. Why do I have to go to anyone but you? Will you set up the foundation for me?"

"Gil's your lawyer, Ethelinda. And a very competent one. He can set up a foundation at the drop of a hat."

"But I want you to be associated with it somehow. I want you to help me."

"Don't you worry. I'll always be here to help you. You can call me any time, day or night. And do you know something, Ethelinda? I feel closer to you right now than I do to my own mother."

The old girl looked startled for a moment, and I

wondered if I had gone too far. But then she seized my hand in both of her old brown ones.

"Oh, Robert, I want to believe you. I really do."

And why should she not have? What I had said was nothing but the truth. I loved Ethelinda for herself and for what she could do for me. I loved her more than I loved my own mother, who had such little faith in me. I loved her more than I had ever loved Sylvia, who might have killed me had her aim with that glass been better. I think at that moment I loved Ethelinda better than anyone in the world except Alice. What do people think that "real" love is made of?

I returned to the office and called Alice to ask if I could come home that night. After a long pause she said she had no food for supper.

"I'll take you out!" I cried exultantly. "I'll take you to the most expensive restaurant in town."

· 21 ·

IN THE NEXT SIX WEEKS the merger talks were resumed between my firm and Gil Arnheim's. They were largely conducted between the two principal partners. Gil and I seemed to understand each other as much in what we didn't say as in what we did. When he asked me if I would be willing to serve on the board of Ethelinda's new foundation, I said that he, as her lawyer, would be a more suitable choice, and when he told me that she had suggested I look over his draft of her new will, I insisted that I had no desire to interfere with his practice. He then agreed to "Arnheim, Buttrick & Service" as the name of the new firm and accorded me a percentage of the net profits equal to his own. A floor in his building directly over the Arnheim offices became available, and we promptly optioned it. The gods themselves seemed in favor of our merger, physical as well as legal.

It appeared, in fact, that my only difficulty would be

in telling Alice. Our reconciliation had so far been easy
and comfortable, and our daughters were sublimely
happy over it. But what would happen when Alice discovered that the merger, which I had assured her had
been abandoned, was now about to be achieved, and at
the cost of the resignation of two of my partners, one of
whom, Peter Stubbs, enjoyed her particular admiration?

I decided to use Douglas Hyde as my ambassador to
Alice.

"She'll have heard bad things about Arnheim," I
warned him.

"From whom? Peter?"

"Perhaps. And from me, too. That first day I went
to see her and ask for a reconciliation I'm afraid I really
shot my mouth off. She's going to think I never meant
it when I said she'd be my conscience. But, honestly,
Doug, I did!"

"I'm sure you meant it, Bob. For that hour, anyway.
What do you want me to tell her?"

"Tell her I have to do this thing for the sake of my
partners."

"Including Peter and Oz Burley?"

"Well, Peter's rich and can afford to be picky. And
Oz is a screwball. Even Alice ought to be able to see
that. Tell her what this will mean financially to the
others. Break it down to dollars and cents. Tell her what
it will mean to you, to your wife and six kids. Hell, it
isn't as if we were signing up with crooks. These men
are rated AVS in *Martindale's!*"

Douglas agreed at last, reluctantly, to give it a try,

and he came home with me tonight to have a drink with
Alice. He is in the living room with her right now,
deciding my fate as I am writing this in the den.

And now I come to a final matter. I think I am going
to discontinue this journal. I believe that to some extent
it has constituted a kind of muffled dialogue between
myself and Alice. I have written down all the things I
couldn't tell her or that she couldn't or wouldn't understand. My yellow pages have formed a useful catharsis
for all my resentment of her persistent unfairness to me.
But now that I am faced with the prospect, or at least the
hope, of our permanent accord, I have begun to wonder
if I may not be doing myself some actual harm by so
carefully recording my acts and then attributing motives
to them. Am I trying to be my own god? My own
creator? I feel that I know what sort of a being Robert
Service is until he becomes a character on the page before
me. And then he seems to take on a different personality.
Is it because I have drawn him too well or too ill?

At the end of *Marius* Pater arranges a semiconversion
to Christianity to give his hero a final solution in his
search of philosophies. But as Pater never quite believed
in anything but beautiful words and artifacts, he could
not bear to bring Marius all the way to God, and he
allowed him a death by disease as opposed to a threatened
martyrdom. What would he have done for me?

A semiconversion? Why not? I may, in giving up my
journal, rejoin my fellow men. If I act and look like a
"nice guy," will I not be one? Quite as much as *you,
hypocrite lecteur, mon semblable, mon frère!* Oh, yes,

for if there should ever be a reader of this page, it would
be such a one. It would have to be such a one, for there
are no others — except perhaps Mr. Hawkins and, in her
best moments, Alice.

Will there be anything left of Robert Service if I *do*,
in the end, become what Alice would like me to be? Ah,
but will there be anything left of Alice? I shall have had
my revenge or my redemption. Perhaps there is no
difference.

Well, it's over now. Douglas has left and Alice has gone
to change her dress. We are going out once again to an
expensive restaurant, but not to celebrate the merger.
We have something quite different to celebrate.

Not that Alice was easy with me. After she had closed
the door behind Doug, she came back and took a rather
formal stand before the fireplace. It was not the first time
she had done this.

"Last year I might have reconsidered the whole question of our reconciliation after hearing what Doug has
just told me. But now I think I have reached the point
where I may be able to accept you for what you are. As
Margaret Fuller accepted the universe. Do you remember what Carlyle said when he heard that? 'By Gad,
she'd better!' "

I looked at her in silent consternation. Who was this
new grave, sarcastic Alice?

"Anyway," she continued, "could I ever have reasonably expected you to be other than you are?"

"Is that so bad a thing?"

"No. And, anyway, perhaps your thesis is correct. Perhaps you *are* like everyone else. And I'm the one who's all along been crazy."

"Not crazy. I never called you that, Alice."

"You only thought it. But that's all right. I never minded your thinking it. And now I'm going to have something else to think about besides you and me and the girls."

I jumped to my feet in excitement as I took in the meaning of her smile. "You couldn't know that already, could you?"

"It's been more than a month, you know. I'm pretty sure." She allowed me to embrace her. "Oh, Bob," she murmured in a more feeling tone as she suddenly clasped my head and stared into my eyes, "it's just what we need to keep us from thinking too closely about each other for a while. Have we been becoming morbid?"

A son at last! For, of course, it will have to be a son after what I have gone through. I am very happy, and don't I deserve to be? The gods are with me, after all.